Kei Matsushima

Kei is a psychiatrist and writer. He was born on Iki-island,
Nagasaki Prefecture in 1974.

He now lives and works in Tokyo. He was awarded the
Prada Feltrinelli Prize 2016.

JN119635

Kei Matsushima

Sunlight

Translated from the Japanese by
Richard Pedlingham, Etsuko Kamibeppu

梓書院
Azusashoin

Azusashoin
3-2-1 Chiyo, Hakata-ku,
Fukuoka-shi, Fukuoka 812-0044,
Japan

Sunlight was first published as *Yoko* in 2018
First published by Azusashoin in 2024

ISBN:978-4-87035-783-9

Printed by LaboNetwork

www.azusashoin.com

Introduction

Writer Kei Matsushima was born into a family of doctors who carried out and still carry out their practice on the small island of Iki, 85 kilometers from Fukuoka, southern Japan. The island was the destination of his summer holidays and his childhood playground.

Returning to the island as an adult, in an attempt to catch the essence of the island, Kei carried out a series of interviews with islanders who had some sort of connection with his family. By listening to and recording the stories, he managed to piece together a series of short stories, which in turn became this book.

The stories are sometimes succinct and to the point and other times meandering and magical. They are always charming. They provide a matter of fact insight to life on and off the island. They depict family ties, the rigors of arranged marriage, childhood hopes and dreams, separation, adoption, growing old, war and death. All set amongst fishing boats, smuggling, rice fields, sandy beaches and sunlight.

A delightful step into the recent past.

Richard Pedlingham

Contents

Sunlight

Although my family lived in a city on the mainland, my mother told me later that my grandparents, more precisely my grandmother's purpose was to introduce a taste of island life to my brother. They wanted to instill into him that as the first-born son he would have to return to the island after becoming a doctor. He was two years older than me. We used to spend our summer holidays at my grandparents on Iki-island. My grandfather was a local doctor and had a clinic on a hill overlooking the port. I would spend a full month of summer on the island, catching beetles and swimming in the sea. My mother used to see my brother off with tears in her eyes. She made me quite aware of her sadness, her first son was being taken away from her. She seems to forget that I was also being sent off to the island, but I was just tagging along.

My grandmother's plan was a success. My brother retuned to the island to work at my father's hospital the year before last and became known as "Junior". His wife and daughter continue to live in Fukuoka-city and he works on the island during the week and on weekends returns to the city. His only daughter, my niece, goes to a ballet school, freeing her from any duty on the island.

My grandparents had a live-in maid. She did everything in the house, cooking, washing, cleaning, and shopping. They lived in a two-storied Japanese style house connected to the clinic by a corridor.

My grandfather spent most of his time in his study when he was not consulting the patients. It was a small corner room on the second floor, filled with brushes and paper for calligraphy. I was told that he was a highly regarded calligrapher on the island. Quite a few local signs seen at the parks and public facilities were written by him.

He wrote throughout the year on a large desk in the middle of his study. I was told to go upstairs and tell Grandfather that dinner was ready. Opening the door, I would see my grandfather's straight back, he was engrossed in his writing.

I did not realize until later in life that this study, an eight-tatami-mat room, was my grandfather's sanctuary. He had been married into the family, changed his name, and knew his place. The true head of the house was my grandmother.

My grandmother who was a daughter of a general practitioner had an elder sister but no brothers. A young man from the island who was studying literature at a university in Tokyo was chosen to be her future husband. He was told, "You won't be able to make a living through literature. I want you to go to medical school and I will pay for the school expenses. Will you marry my daughter and become a doctor?" He became a doctor.

At my grandparents' house, every meal was prepared by the maid. Living on an island meant abundant fresh fish on the table. Meat and vegetables were also grown locally.

For some reason my grandfather used to have his breakfast early, alone. The menu was always the same. Sliced-bread with strawberry jam and warm milk. The bread was not even toasted. He would fold the bread with jam in two and dip it into the milk. Every day, day after day.

One day I asked him while he was eating. "Grandfather, you really enjoy your breakfast, don't you?" He gazed at me with an awkward expression.

We were alone, as my grandmother had just left.

"Actually, I would prefer to have a regular breakfast, dried sardines, some miso-soup, and a bowl of white rice."

I was dumbfounded. I had always assumed he must have loved his breakfast because he ate it every day. I was puzzled and could not quite understand, but at the same time I somehow felt I should drop the subject, and also felt that I shouldn't mention our conversation to anyone else. In fact, I have never brought it up until now.

The only housework my grandmother did was preparing Grandfather's breakfast in order to maintain to others that her husband was properly cared for. She did not know how to cook at all. Putting jam on bread, and warming milk were the only things she was able to do.

No one expected her to be a diligent wife, nor criticized her. For the most part she avoided any social life. She did not need to make excuses to anyone.

*

Coming back from the beach, before entering the beach-house, you had to clean the sand off your feet by first rubbing one foot against the other in the foot bath, then dry them by stamping on the mat. Only after this were you allowed to step onto the tatami mats. The water in the foot bath was used by many people, and only rarely changed. It was filthy. The bath mat for drying feet was worse still. It had been used over and over again and I doubted if it really served any purpose at all.

At the beginning of each summer, I could not bring myself to put my feet into the foot bath. Instead I went to a close-by water-tap and washed my feet with running water. Leaving wet footprints on the tatami mat, I hurried to my uncle and aunt, who gave me a fresh towel to dry my feet. There was always a watermelon waiting for us.

The only other people who washed their feet under the tap were young women visiting on holiday. I felt ashamed. After some days, I took the plunge and soaked my feet in the foot bath and jumped onto the dirty bath mat. I didn't care anymore.

Every year I went through this ritual to become a proper island boy, indomitable. Giving a contemptuous glance to those visitors washing under the tap, I bit into the watermelon and gazed at the beach. Dazzling white sand. Sunlight reflecting off the waves. The sound of cicada from the pine trees behind the house. Occasional cries of herons.

Now whenever I return to the island in summer, I go down to the beach. The silence is replaced by a constant roar of Jet-skis. The sound of Reggae beats from a concert being held for the tourists on a nearby open stage.

Whenever I miss those summer days of my youth, I try to visit out of season. No engine noise and no speakers, just the very distinct sound of waves breaking on the shore.

*

My grandfather had a chauffeur, who was hired to drive him to his patient's homes. He also took care of my grandfather and was a playmate of mine. Hirakawa and I would sumo-wrestle, play at being samurai, play catch. He also taught me a card game called Menko. He would take me to catch beetles in the woods behind the house early in the morning. He knew the woods well and the best place to find them.

I often saw him washing my grandfather's car in front of the garage. Shirtless, he would hose down the car, and polish it with a sponge. The bumpers and the wheels sparkled in the summer sunlight. Once he finished his job, he would hose himself down. Then he would use a scrubbing brush on his arms and shoulders. He had a dragon tattoo that stretched from his shoulder to his elbow.

"Young master, this doesn't come off however hard I scrub it."

Every time he washed the car, he would scrub away at the tattoo.

By the time I entered junior high school, he had quit his driving job and opened a small Ramen shop at the end of the port. It soon went out of business. He started a yakitori-shop. It closed. Then a takoyaki-shop. It closed, too. He tried his hand at everything. He sold grilled squid at the summer festival, Umegae-mochi in front of the shrine on New Year's Day. It was much later that I learned there was a name for people like Hirakawa 'Carny'. Hirakawa's drinking habit sometimes led him into trouble. As he got older, he had a problem with his liver. Eventually he died of a cerebral hemorrhage.

*

I have a particular memory even though I am not entirely sure if it was just a dream.

One evening, my grandfather came home late after a medical association meeting or something like that. I went out the front door and down to the bottom of the hill to meet him. "Look, look," he exclaimed and started to tap dance under the street light. He was wearing a linen suit and leather shoes, and danced light-footed like Fred Astaire in the spotlight.

I just stared at him with wide-eyed wonder. After dancing for a good while he put his forefinger on his lips and went into the house. That was the only time I ever saw him dance.

My grandfather died of aortic dissection when I was a university student. At his Hatsubon (the first bon festival after death), I brought up the subject of his dancing. "Dancing? What nonsense! What are you talking about?" Everyone laughed. Did I really see him dance, or was I just dreaming? I never really thought about it again until the other day when I was talking to Mrs. Mawatari, a 97-year-old neighbor. For some reason I asked her whether she had seen my grandfather dance. With no hesitation, she replied,

"Yes, yes, of course, he was a great tap dancer. Perhaps I shouldn't mention this to you, but since both the doctor and his wife have passed away, I'm sure they wouldn't mind. You see, when the doctor was young, he was quite stylish, debonair, and warm-hearted. But he changed a lot."

It is impossible to talk about my grandfather without thinking how much his life was affected by the existence of my grandmother. I am glad that seeing him dance under the street light was not just my imagination, but on the other hand I feel a pang of sadness. In time all things fade, even memories fade.

*

There was no sandy beach near the port town where my grandparents lived. We often went to the closest beach on the other side of the island, about 20 minutes away by car. Hirakawa used to drive us there and bring us back. On our way, we crossed the largest plain on the island. Rice paddies spread out from both sides of the road. Green ears of rice swayed in the wind. Although it was a familiar scene for us, Hirakawa would proudly repeat many times, "Look at those fields. Have you ever seen anything like them?"

Now, driving along the same road, we can still see green rice fields, but only on the right hand side. On the left stands the Haranotsuji Ruins which were discovered and then excavated slowly over time and designated as National historical site some ten years ago. In the hope of attracting tourists a row of ancient houses were reconstructed. In a way I am sad that the wide open space no longer exists, but I have no right to complain.

Recently I learned that in the past there were sandy beaches next to the port, white fine sand stretched out like a fan for two to three kilometers both sides of the river mouth. I imagined the ancient people who lived where the ruins now stand catching fish on the beach.

In 1950s, the beaches disappeared. My great-grandfather, who was a doctor and also a member of the local assembly, was a part of a planning committee who decided to reclaim the land for rice. Unfortunately the soil was not good enough, so in the end most of the land was used to grow tobacco. Looking across the vast tobacco field, I felt the irreversible path of progress. How beautiful the town would be if there was still a beach there.

Alongside the tobacco field there is a bus stop named 'Yokohama', literally on the beach.

Passengers squinted as the dazzling sun reflected off the sand. In the distance waves glistened. A barge advanced slowly towards the mainland. A flight of black-tailed gulls swooped through the air.

There is another thing that I recently learned.

Hirakawa, in his later years, needed to be nursed because of the aftereffects of a cerebral hemorrhage. His body was paralysed, and his disposition was affected becoming violent towards his wife and children. I was told that he repeatedly called out my name, endlessly recounting to his own son his memories of those summer days, catching beetles and sumo wrestling with me.

As Hirakawa's life deteriorated, I was enjoying myself in the city to the point that I had forgotten his existence.

*

My grandmother outlived my grandfather by twenty years, and spent her last few years at my father's hospital. In her later years she was bedridden and was not able to communicate. I was a heartless grandson. I rarely went to see her at the hospital. At her wake, a nurse enquired, "When did you last come to see her?" I could not remember when.

At my grandparents my brother and I slept side by side in the same room, a Japanese style room on the second floor. One night I wet my bed. Just like you might see in a comic book, I dreamed of going to the lavatory and woke up to find myself in a puddle. It was three o'clock at night. My brother was fast asleep.

My bedding and pyjamas were all soaked. I went to my grandparents' room and woke up my grandmother.

"Oh, dear," she said and helped me change my clothes, and remade my bed. I could not go back to sleep. So I went back to her again. She said, "Bring your pillow."

My grandfather was snoring with his mouth wide open. I put my pillow between my grandparents. My grandmother lay on her side resting on her elbow, looking in my direction. She did not say anything.

I said to her, "Will you sing me a song?" She was at a loss. She could not sing any children's songs, so she had a go at singing Enka but soon gave up. After some thought, she started to sing "Country Bus", a comical song of the Showa period.

The words and melody of the song suited our situation perfectly. We both giggled.

"Please sing it again", I begged her over and over.

We both felt the kind of affection normally associated between a grandmother and a grandson, and both felt a sense of relief. Occasionally when we were alone, I noticed her singing the song to herself. My one fond memory of my grandmother.

*

The beach was always deserted after five. It wasn't evening yet, but the sun was beginning to go down. The owner of the beach house and his wife would sit down on a bench in front of the cash register. The student working part time would drag the boats for hire back onto the beach. My brother and I would join him to help. After that we would race each other to the bench. The owner would give us unsold rice balls.

"The sea is at its most gorgeous in the evening, isn't it?"

Listening to his wife's favourite phrase, I would gaze at the coming and going of the waves.

I am going to spend tomorrow too at the beach.

A Barge

How long has it been since my great-aunt passed away?

I could easily find this out by just calling my father. However I thought it was better to avoid this topic because he had just had an operation on the cancer that had spread from his bladder to his kidney. But why on earth was I thinking about my great-aunt? Probably it was the very fact my father was ill. By calling and asking him, he would sense what was really on my mind.

My great-aunt lived in the main house. So we called her Big-granny. She was my grandmother's elder sister. The main house was at the foot of a hill, about 15 minutes away by car from my grandparents. It was a big country house surrounded by forest. Her late father's clinic still stood next to the house.

After the death of my great-aunt, the house remained unoccupied for a while. Then, a man who made fishing rods and a retired university professor from Tokyo wanted to rent a part of the house. They must have been looking forward to a new start in the country, but soon they learned that country life involved centipedes, mamushi pit vipers, nosy neighbors, and gossip. It took less than one year for them to return to Tokyo. An uninhabited house grows old quickly and it is now almost in ruins.

My brother and I spent our entire summer holiday at my grandparents. My parents, however, joined us for only a few days during the Bon festival. And it was customary for my family to pay a visit to the main house when they were on the island.

*

Entering from the back of the house, you would pass through an earthen floored porch into another small room of about eight tatami-mats.

Big-granny put down a blue tin car she was holding and went to the kitchen to get us barley tea. My parents and Big-granny started to talk. My brother and I soon lost interest, and so finishing up the tea, went outside. There was a well behind the house. We had a lot of fun playing with the old fashioned pump, splashing water everywhere. Then Big-granny would call us through the living room window.

"I have some cake for you. Come and eat."

It was already cut in its usual place on a big plate on a low table. Competing with each other we ate as fast as possible.

"Don't rush. I have some more," she laughed.

Sitting by the window, and moving the tin car to and fro, she said,

"Don't you want pickles? How about some soda?"

We all sat on the veranda looking at the garden. Yellow canna flowers and pink crape myrtles were in bloom. I scratched my mosquito-bitten arm. Big-granny stood up saying, "I will go and fetch some ointments and mosquito-repellent."

In the corner of the veranda, the blue car was waiting for her return.

Big-granny lost her son in a motor bike accident. He was only 25 years old. The tin car was his childhood treasure. Big-granny carried it about with her throughout her life. Motor bikes were banned forever in our family. I have been told this repeatedly since my childhood, and the same rule still applies now.

*

My first car was a used Nissan Sunny. The second summer after entering university, I took it to the island on a ferry. After driving around the island, I visited Big-granny. I parked the car in the thatched garage which used to be a stable. It was not the Bon festival, so I am not really sure why I went to see her that evening.

Just like in my childhood, she offered me soda. All the windows and doors were tightly closed to keep insects out. It was cold, the air conditioner was on full. Even so I could hear the evening cicadas.

"I somehow like the sound of evening cicadas," said I.

"Oh, do you?" said she, "but isn't it a lonely sound?"

We watched TV together for a while. High school baseball games were on. As the sun set and evening grew dim, she began to talk about her life, her past before she became Big-granny.

The fact she had had a past and a childhood came to me as a surprise. I had never imagined her in any other way except my great-aunt. She even had her own name.

Her name was Machiko.

*

At the age of four, Machiko boarded a passenger boat to Iki-island from the mainland with her parents. Her father was a police officer, and was being transferred to the police substation on the island.

In those days, the depth of the water at the island's port was too shallow for the passenger boats to come alongside the pier. So they were anchored offshore, and passengers had to change to small barges that took them to the sandy beach.

It was a clear summer afternoon. The barge advanced slowly on the calm sea. The strong sun reflected off the ocean blinded Machiko. She raised her hands to protect her eyes as she looked towards the bow and into the distance. The white sandy beach spread as far as she could see.

Before the bow reached the beach, a boatman jumped off, making the barge sway. Machiko grabbed the arm of her father, who was sitting next to her. Her brother held on to his sister, and the sister held the hem of her mother's kimono. Both her father and mother tried to keep their balance, laughing and saying, "Be careful! Look out!" Carried or helped by the boatman, they made it to the shore. Damp sand gave way softly under their feet. Lapping waves then washed away their footprints.

Machiko's father was a good and honest man, and soon became part of the local community. He became known as 'Bobby'. He had almost nothing to do. Crimes were very rare, and even if there were any, they were usually settled within the community. The police substation was situated inland from the port where the farmland began. It also served as their house. The family enjoyed a relaxed country life.

One day Machiko found a private road turning to the right on the way to the mountain. There was a wooden one-story house at the end of the road. The walls were painted white, and on the glass door was gold lettering. She walked up to the door and touched the lettering, a woman in a long sleeved white apron came out.

"You are alone?"

"Yes," Machiko nodded.

"What's the matter? Are you hurt?"

"What does it say?" Machiko with an inquisitive tilt of her bobbed haired head pointed at the lettering on the glass door.

The woman smiled and said, "It says Sangenjaya Clinic."

The sliding door inside the house opened and a man in white came towards them.

"Whose child are you?" he asked and crouched down beside Machiko.

"I'm Katsuragi Machiko."

"Ah, you are Bobby's daughter."

He had a stethoscope hanging around his neck.

"Is this a hospital?"

"That's right. I am the doctor, and she is the nurse."

At that moment a horse neighed somewhere. Machiko's eyes widened with amazement.

"There's a horse over there. Do you want to see it?"

The doctor took Machiko's hand, and led her through the house to the back door, which led to a courtyard with a pond. To the right a stable housed a chestnut horse used for calling on patients. Next to it stood a barn with two black cows. He held Machiko up and she patted the horse's neck.

From that time on Machiko frequently visited the clinic to see the horse. The doctor simply doted on her. He took her to the stable between seeing patients, and taught her how to make music by blowing a blade of grass. He invited her into their two-storied house and gave her some sweets. Machiko became attached to him. She loved to draw pictures or play with beanbags on his lap.

Seeing some women also wearing white aprons, Machiko asked,

"Nurses?," making them laugh aloud.

"No. They are maids," replied the doctor.

When the doctor was busy, the maids took care of her.

Once when Machiko was playing with them in the wooden floored room next to the kitchen, they suddenly all stood up and left hurriedly in different directions. She looked up and saw a woman in a kimono with her hair up. She did not smile at all, and turned around and left. The maids called her 'Ma'am.' Ma'am was always dressed in a beautiful kimono, and always had a stern look on her face.

The doctor took good care of Machiko's family, too. He helped them in many ways, sending fish and rice, and inviting them to the festivals. Thus the family was not exposed to the tougher elements of island life and the hardship of autumn and winter.

Bobby was detailed to be transferred early spring of the following year. The doctor had become so fond of Machiko that he did not want her to leave.

One evening, with a lantern in his hand the doctor came to visit the family at the substation. There was nobody at the station, so he went round to the back entrance of the house and rang the doorbell. He was welcomed by all the members of the family.

"I'm sorry for visiting you so late. I wanted to have a

word with you."

He looked unusually serious. He sat at the low dining table, sipped a mouthful of tea, and said,

"Mrs. Katsuragi, would you do me a favour? There is something I would like to discuss with your husband. Could you kindly leave us alone for a while?"

As soon as they were alone, he straightened himself and said, "Could I have Machiko as my adopted daughter?"

Bobby was astonished. As the proposal was so sudden, he was at a loss for words. Not knowing what to say next, both of them sat there and just gazed at pickles on the table. After a long pause, the doctor said, "Please think about it." Then he left.

Bobby was torn, everything considered. It may not be a bad proposal for Machiko's future. Not being able to decide himself, he confronted Machiko.

"Do you want to be the child of the doctor?"

"Yes." Machiko nodded.

Machiko, held high by the doctor, waved at her parents and her brother and sister as they left on a barge. Her father and mother kept their eyes fixed on their daughter. The barge slowly advanced towards a waiting passenger boat anchored offshore. Not taking her eyes off the boat, Machiko uttered, "Doctor?"

"From now on you must call me Father."

Machiko could not decide whether she should call Ma'am Mother. Nothing had changed since their first meeting. She was still cold to her. Perhaps she could not help it. She had her own problems. The main role of wives in those days was to bear children, and in case of failure take all the blame. Ma'am's name was Kie. The doctor's name was Yasutaro. In contrast to Kie, he was a straightforward man.

One day Machiko gained a sister, or rather a sister suddenly appeared. The suckling child had narrow eyes and thin lips.

"Naomi, you are really lucky, aren't you?"

The maids were trying to calm the baby who moved restlessly on the futon. Machiko, standing in the wooden floored room, observed them from afar.

"Now that she is adopted into this family, she has nothing to worry about."

"Whose child is she?"

"The Akais in Kawamukai-village. In Kawamukai the rice harvest has been very poor for many years."

"They are really suffering. Every family is really poor."

"When it comes to being poor, my family isn't an exception. Ah, I wish I were also adopted."

With this the maids burst into laughter.

Surprisingly Kie smiled in front of Naomi. Machiko wondered why Ma'am adored her so much. Is it because Naomi was still an infant?

Five years later when Machiko became ten, she found out why Ma'am had constantly shown favoritism towards Naomi. Machiko was quiet and serious whereas Naomi was selfish and malicious. Naomi was just like Ma'am.

When Yasutaro gave both of them pocket money, Machiko saved it not wasting it on useless things. On the other hand Naomi would spend it all the very same day.

Ma'am would look at Machiko coldly and say, "What an unlovable child you are!"

And then turning to her sister with a smile, she would say, "Naomi, you are so much sweeter. Children should be children," as she gave her more money.

It was always the same. For example, Machiko did well at school, whereas Naomi did poorly. Even so Machiko was never praised. Having good marks was not regarded as endearing.

Why did Yasutaro, who did not have any children of his own, adopt two girls, and no boy? Suppose he adopted a boy, and the boy didn't turn out how he expected, then it would immediately mean the end of the family lineage. He could find a doctor to succeed him but then he would not be an inheritor in the real sense. What about the family lineage?

In that sense, adopting a girl first and then finding a doctor to be her husband was the most certain way of gaining an heir. Yasutaro was a tactician.

Machiko wanted to continue her studies, but Kie coldly stated, "That's not necessary." Yasutaro's mind was occupied with the process of finding her husband. Not just anyone. Being a doctor was not enough. The most important thing was a doctor who would take over his clinic and live on the island. He visited a local school and talked to the school master and had interviews with some of the brightest students. Nakazawa Tadao was among them, and obviously stood out from the others. He had hungry eyes.

"To marry your daughter?"

The interview was held in the headmaster's office. Tadao

sat on the leather sofa with his legs crossed. Yasutaro was impressed by his fearless attitude.

"To marry her and continue my clinic, this is the condition."

Yasutaro assured him that he would pay all the necessary expenses to go to medical school. Tadao listened intently, and decided his future there and then.

Only after everything was arranged and decided, was Machiko informed. Tadao was an attractive man from a neighboring town. She accepted her fate obediently. In fact she was rather pleased. Tadao had a somewhat crude manner which seemed to young Machiko to be manly.

Tadao successfully passed the examination to enter a newly opened medical school in Tokyo. This was as expected considering his school grades. It was also known that at a new school money talked. His fiancée, Machiko stayed on the island, and visited him in Tokyo twice a year. Tadao was not particularly welcoming, but at night he made love to her. He lived in a neat rented-house, which he furnished well.

After making love, he would smoke a cigarette in bed. Then looking around the room, he would say to her, grinning, "You are lucky, aren't you?"

Or he would say to Machiko as if sneering at her, "I wonder what your father's intention is by sending you here." He would snort in self-deprecation.

Machiko wondered the same thing. She was there with main purpose of protecting her father's investment and to remind Tadao of his agreement and bind him to it, just like the gold watch on the desk and medical books on the shelf. She thought that he along with all the other islanders probably knew that she was an adopted child.

Still, she looked forward to going to Tokyo. She felt an indescribable happiness when she boarded the barge. Tadao might be a bad man, but he had all the charm particular to that of a playboy. Machiko having been brought up in comfortable circumstances was unable to resist.

Tadao graduated from the university and quickly acquired a medical licence. Machiko waited for him on the island, but heard nothing from him. Yasutaro sent a telegram to Tadao's address, but received no reply. Could he be drinking in celebration with his friends? Tadao's parents who lived on the island said that they too had heard nothing from him.

So Machiko went to Tokyo to see what was going on. From Tokyo Station she went directly to his house, but he was not there. She returned to his house in vain until she finally asked his landlord to open the door. Although the furniture was still there, she soon realized his other belongings such as medical books and clothing were gone from the shelf and wardrobe. Having acquired his medical licence, he simply disappeared.

Machiko spent some weeks in Tokyo. She visited the office of his medical school only to find out that they had lost all contact with him. The clerk in the office told her that many of their graduates usually stayed to work as interns at their university hospital, but not all of them did so. Some would return to their hometown to be trained at the local hospital, others would not even inform them of their whereabouts. "As long as you have a medical licece, anything is possible," he added.

"Return home," was the reply to Machiko's telegram

from her father.

Machiko cleared away the furniture that Tadao had left, and paid the remaining rent. The landlord told her that another woman used to visit him, and he had probably ran away with her. She could not quite grasp why he had told her this. He looked bemused, so she deduced it was probably out of kindness.

After returning to the island, Machiko confined herself to her house for some time. The news that Tadao had betrayed Machiko, and in turn Yasutaro, and disappeared spread quickly. On a small island scandal reaches everybody's ears in no time.

Shortly after that, Naomi started to say, "I want to have a go at Tokyo life." Kie accepted her request with no hesitation. However, Yasutaro would only let her go on two conditions. Firstly she must go to college. Secondly, after graduation she should return to the island. She was accepted into a pharmaceutical college, again a newly opened school.

Machiko was envious of Naomi. Her sister was allowed to go away to study. It was not just envy. She had a kind of begrudging frustration at the way Naomi lived her life.

On the day Naomi left for Tokyo, Machiko, together with her parents, went to see her off. Naomi sitting on the barge with her back towards them did not even bothered to glance back in their direction.

Not so long after that, Machiko was informed of the fact that another engagement had been arranged for her.

It was an intern living in Kurume City. His name was

Fuminori. He was originally from the island, but was adopted by a farmer in the suburbs of Kurume when he was a child. He had wanted to open a clinic on the island. Hearing about Fuminori, Yasutaro was quick in action and arrangements were made immediately. Yasutaro would support them while he was training. After finishing the training period, he should return to the island and take over the clinic. These were the conditions Yasutaro imposed.

His appearance was that of a country man. Machiko found him 'unrefined and unsophisticated', but he seemed to her to be pleasant, gentle, mild-mannered, quiet and simple.

Machiko started to live with Fuminori in Kurume. Their wedding and the reception were to be held after he completed his training and returned to the island. He was to enter Machiko's family, and perhaps Yasutaro was somehow cautious. Their new house was one-storied, and rather inappropriately large for a doctor in training. Needless to say, it was provided by Yasutaro. What surprised Machiko was that Fuminori accepted the financial support from his father-in-law to be, with no hesitation. He tailored new suits and bought an imported watch, sending the bills to Yasutaro. She was aware that this was a part of the condition of their marriage, but still Machiko felt so disappointed seeing him taking full advantage of the situation. She was confused by the gap between his image and behavior.

I am after all just an intermediary. She despised herself, and started to loose confidence. Fuminori was thick set. In fact Machiko sometimes thought about Tadao's sinewy body in the midst of their love-making.

Since she was adopted by Yasutaro, she had never lived off

the island for any extended period of time, and of course she was experiencing being newly-wed for the first time. Perhaps this is what people call happiness, she thought. Although in Kurume there was no sea, it had a big river called the Chikugo running through its suburb. Machiko sometimes strolled alone along the banks. Looking at the river she thought perhaps time also flows slowly like the water.

About a year had passed when one day, out of the blue, something happened to Fuminori.

His appearance changed. He became restless. He started peeping outside through a narrow opening between the doors. He would utter, "They are following me," or "The police are watching me."

One day, looking at Machiko with bloodshot eyes, he shouted loudly.

"Who are you? You are not Machiko. You are just posing as Machiko."

With this, he dashed out of the house.

Machiko was terrified. Struck with fear, she sank down in the corner of the kitchen, shaking helplessly, holding her knees.

Fuminori was yelling out unintelligibly in the middle of a busy street when the police finally caught him. The police, determining there was something wrong with him, took him to the same university hospital where he worked. Machiko rushed to the hospital as soon as she was informed. Fuminori was detained in a prison-like ward. She was shocked by what she saw. He was roaring out and banging himself against the iron railing.

Yasutaro came rushing to Machiko's aid. Again, he was

quick in action. "Return to the island," he told Machiko and sent her back the very same day. He stayed on in Kurume for a few more days and did what had to be done. Whenever Machiko tried to ask him about Fuminori, he only repeated, "Please be patient."

He sent a representative to Kurume with detailed instructions. After some weeks, Machiko's marriage, and consequently Fuminori's plans were annulled. Machiko felt sorry for Fuminori, but Yasutaro clearly stated, "It cannot be helped. He is not fit to take over the clinic." The house where they had lived in Kurume was emptied by his representative, and Machiko never returned there. The image of mentally deranged Fuminori stayed with her. Eventually she heard the rumour that Fuminori had hanged himself.

A suitor had been arranged for Naomi, who was now living in Tokyo. It was a young man named Hiroki, who after finishing high school on the island, was studying literature in a university in Tokyo. He was known to be a brilliant student. Yasutaro singled him out to be Naomi's future husband. He invited Hiroki to his house when he returned home in the summer of that year.

"You cannot live on literature. Why don't you become a doctor? You can still enjoy literature on the side. I will provide you with enough money for studies and your living expenses. You shall have your own clinic and a house."

Hiroki, in the end, was persuaded and accepted the offer. He entered the medical department of the Kyushu Imperial University.

Machiko sadly realised that she was now completely alone,

and it was Naomi who was going to help provide Yasutaro with the successor he so wanted. She could not help but think that she was now regarded useless by everyone including maids, and even the traders who came to their house, and of course Ma'am. She felt hollow, worthless, empty inside.

Hiroki returned to the island shortly after completing his medical course. Yasutaro bought land on a hill near the port to build a clinic and a house for him. Although Japan was in the middle of the pacific war, fortunately Iki-island suffered no air raids apart from the occasional machine gun attack. It was forgotten by the world.

Of course young men were called up to the war and some were killed. Air-raid shelters were constructed at various points on the island.

Hiroki became involved in his own private battle within the Imperial University Hospital.

After duly graduating from the medical department, he trained specifically to become a surgeon. Around the beginning of the war, there was awareness of America's might, and worrying murmurs were heard concerning Japan's future. Soon, however, the rumours begun to disappear as people became nervous, as saying anything that discreditted the country was regarded as treason.

Towards the end of the war, Hiroki overheard conversations about live human experiments that were to be performed on American war prisoners.

He did not take it seriously at first, but over time more concrete contents leaked out. The head of the department would lead the plans to perform vivisection. Hiroki was dumbfounded. Are they serious? Are they really going to perform such acts? He shuddered at the mass hysteria brought about by war and the madness of academism. He became tormented. He decided to leave the hospital and did so by lying that his father-in-law suddenly passed away, so he had to return to take over the clinic on the island. He would have been punished if they found out that it was a lie. Fortunately they suspected nothing and he safely returned to the island.

The Imperial University carried out the experiments. After the war, this barbarous act was criminalized, and those involved were severely punished.

Iki-island lies half way between Kyushu and the Korean Peninsula. Because of its geographical importance, as a precaution, the army built a huge gun tower, the largest in Asia. However, it was later dismantled without ever being used.

Hiroki opened his clinic just before the war ended. While people were suffering and supplies were short all over Japan, a fine clinic was built. When the roof structure was completed, in accordance with the customary practice in Japan, Yasutaro threw down rice cakes from the top of the roof. He could have given his own clinic and house to Hiroki, but he did not do so. Maybe this was in consideration for Machiko, because if he had done so, she would have to leave.

Yasutaro referred many of his patients to Hiroki. He was becoming more interested in politics than practicing medicine. However, he was not thinking of retiring, not in the least. He had no interest in participating in the government. His main interest was to gain power, and more precisely how he could profit from using his power on the island. He became involved with a local civil engineering and construction company. He ran for the local assembly after the war, and successfully became elected.

Like before, Machiko was informed for the third time about the arrangement of her marriage after everything had been decided. Yasutaro placed a picture of the man on the table.

"Sadakichi is not a doctor, but he has just returned from Korea. He was a police officer before. I shall need his help in many ways."

Machiko took the picture in her hand. A short haired man with square jaw was staring straight ahead. Honestly speaking she felt a chill. She thought she saw in his eyes a kind of coldness, but different from that of Ma'am. She soon understood the reason why, as she overheard maids talking about him. He worked in the secret service, stationed in Korea. After the war those working for the secret service were all ousted from public offices. Yasutaro helped him to gain the position of deputy mayor at the town office. The marriage was also a part of Yasutaro's plan.

They started their married life in a newly built one-storied house near the main house. Living with Sadakichi was not as bad as Machiko had expected. It might be because her real father was a police officer. Eventually she was blessed with a son whom they named Genzo.

When she first held Genzo in her arms, she was of course pleased, but it felt slightly unreal. She could hardly believe the fact that the baby she was holding was actually her own.

She was bewildered. Only when she came to accept it to be real, did she feel for the first time in her life that she was also made of flesh and blood.

This must be it, she thought, this must be what people call happiness. At the same time she was overcome by a kind of fear that she had never experienced before. What if she were to loose Genzo? Just by imaging that made her blood drain. And thus she learned that happiness was indeed accompanied by fear.

Yasutaro made a plan for a land development project in league with a construction company. It was a big land reclamation project under the pretext of increasing the agricultural land available. Sadakichi lived up to Yasutaro's expectation. He had been involved in conspiracies in the Korean Peninsula, and now he was Yasutaro's right hand man in the town office.

The initial reclamation project began with the estimated completion time of ten years. During this period, Yasutaro was continuously reelected. As the beach disappeared, his power increased. By the time the first project finished, half of the beach was lost.

One day when Machiko was washing vegetables in the kitchen, Hiroki's driver came rushing in.

"I have come to fetch you. Please get ready to go to the clinic."

On the way the driver talking into the rear-view mirror explained to her what had happened.

"The doctor has collapsed, and he is no longer breathing."

Machiko was unable to speak. Instead she remembered the day long ago when Yasutaro held her in his arms as she waved to her parents as they left on a barge.

The car sped along the portside road. The sky and the sea were dazzlingly blue. She saw a passenger boat far off at sea.

Yasutaro lay on a bed in the clinic, his face was already covered with white cloth.

"It was a heart attack," Hiroki mumbled. It was not clear whether he was telling this to everyone or just talking to himself.

The secondary reclamation project which had been planned was continued by Sadakichi with no delay. Sadakichi was also ambitious. He intended to continue where Yasutaro had left off.

One evening, Machiko was in the kitchen. After taking his bath, Sadakichi approached her.

"You know, Father was also adopted into this family by marriage."

Machiko looked at him, startled. But she could not make out the expression on his face. She had long forgotten his previous occupation. Yasutaro was also commandeered by Kie's father, and took over the medical profession. Why had nobody told her? Had everyone on the island known about this? How long had her husband known?

Machiko's life was not her own. She had no control over her destiny and identity. What was she living for? For the sake of a patch-work family held together by thread?

After Yasutaro died, Kie became lifeless. This surprised everyone. Probably no one really understood what Yasutaro's existence had meant to Kie. It remained a mystery to the end. Kie vacated the main house for Machiko and Sadakichi to live, and she shuttered herself away in a smaller house nearby. Machiko, remembering Kie's cold treatment towards her, was puzzled at first. But over time she came to understand; she had grown old, that was all, nothing more.

Machiko herself by then had become the mother of a high school boy and two daughters. The older girl Yoshiko was reliable and the following spring she would enter junior high school. The second daughter Erika was in second grade at elementary school, she was shy and found settling in difficult. Machiko was also quite reserved, and this left her at a loss as to how to help her daughter.

About five years after Yasutaro's death, as the second project was reaching completion, it was Sadakichi's turn to collapse.

"I'm sorry." Hiroki said in a tone that he reserved for a patients' family rather than for his brother-in-law's. Sadakichi had had a cerebral hemorrhage and died on the same bed in the same room as Yasutaro. Machiko looked at her husband's face. His eye lids were not completely closed, they reminded her of a picture of a detained soldier she had once seen.

Her son Genzo had just entered a private university in Fukuoka. Yoshiko was a high school student, and Erika was still at elementary school. Her husband had passed away too young. However when she thought of her life up until now, his death seemed to fall into place. People all die someday. She felt some kind of nostalgia for Tadao, Fuminori, and her two fathers. This was her husband's turn.

However, she was not alone. She had Genzo, Yoshiko, and Erika. Genzo was twenty years old now, but she still marvelled in the miracle of his birth. This in turn gave her a reason to continue her own life. She sometimes went to visit him. From the new concreted port constructed as a part of the reclamation project, which allowed even large-scale passenger ships to come alongside the pier, she went up the gangway and boarded. Barges had long been disused.

Machiko had never believed in God nor Buddha until then. However she began to begrudge them and made them the spearhead of her anger.

It was five years after Sadakichi's death. She was picking weeds in the garden. "Shall I lend you a mower?" offered Mr. Tomita, a gardener. She did not want any help when it came to gardening. She wanted to teach Genzo about trees and flowers in the garden when he returned. And as a matter of fact, she felt a little awkward when Mr. Tomita was around. He was not a bad person, but whenever he saw her, he would talk about Naomi, which annoyed Machiko. Naomi had four children, all boys. She expected one of them would become a doctor and take over their clinic. Machiko seldom saw her sister, but had no real problem with her. They simply did not get along very well. Keeping a distance is the best way, this is what Machiko had learned over the years.

Genzo graduated from the university and stayed on in Fukuoka where he found a job in a trading company. He showed no interest in the medical profession nor wanted to return home. Machiko thought that it was better that way, as she did not want Genzo to become stuck on the island.

Machiko was trying to pick a Takeni-gusa from under the veranda when the telephone rang. Taking off her work gloves, she entered the house. "Hello?" she put the receiver to her ear. The caller first gave his name as so and so from the Hakata Police Station and said, "Your son, Genzo has been in an accident."

Machiko shivered, she was affected by the way he spoke, by the tone of his voice.

"Unfortunately ……,"

Machiko could not breathe. There was silence on the other end of line, the police officer was waiting for her response. She could not find her voice. Words exploded inside her. Please! Forgive me! Wait! God!

Genzo was riding a motorbike on a national road, and missed a curve. The motorbike overturned and he was thrown onto the road landing heavily on his head. He died instantly. She could not accept his death. Something inside Machiko was destroyed forever.

*

It was pitch dark outside. The night in the country is frightfully dark.

"You must be careful on the road," Big-granny said as she took a tin car in her hand.

I had never talked with her this long before. For, to be honest, I had thought she was a little crazy. She looked absent minded and always had the tin car with her. I remember hearing her daughter Erika saying that she sometimes found it difficult to talk with her mother. I might have misunderstood her.

"Do you have anyone you are fond of?" Big-granny suddenly asked me.

"We just split up," I answered. "Is that so?" she began to laugh covering her mouth with her hand.

She took a cup and sipped some tea, and then gazed out of the window. She could see nothing but darkness. Still she kept looking as if searching for something outside. And then she muttered,

"I wish I could see Tadao one more time."

Tadao was the name of her first fiancée. I could not quite make out what she meant by saying that. Was he still alive? Was he the only one who really knew her? Had she been in love with him all these years?

We watched the sports news on TV together and I left her house at midnight. She saw me off at the front door. On my way back it was too dark to see anything beyond the range of the headlight. It seemed the space of nothingness had expanded.

*

How long has it been since Big-granny passed away?

I asked my father when I returned home for New Year.

"Wasn't it seven years ago? The funeral was held at Kogenji-temple. I remember it was pouring with rain."

Was it that long ago? In one sense it somehow felt longer. I just remembered it had rained heavily that day, and the feeling of my mourning suit drenched to my skin. Funerals on the island were in a way celebrations and could easily be mistaken for festivals. Four Buddhist priests in colourful robes danced reading scriptures to the sound of drums and other musical instruments.

"She had lung cancer. It had spread all over her body in the end," said my father. He himself had just had an operation for the removal of his left kidney, but a postop examination the previous week found another cancer in his bladder. He was going to have a polypectomy the following month, but he being a surgeon himself showed no sign of wavering.

I asked him about the lost beach. He told me his childhood memory of summer. A part of the coming-of-age ceremony for the men on Iki-island was to swim across from the beach to another beach in the neighboring town. Every boy who reached to the age of twelve had to go through the ritual. He was then considered to be a man.

The participant would start to swim from the beach accompanied by a barge, with a few older boys in loincloth on board, ready to dive in to help just in case.

When I reached the open sea, the swell of the waves became stronger. I felt very tired, but still kept swimming.

"Hang on! Stick to it! Only a little more!"

I could hear voices from the barge. The sun burned my shoulders. A flying fish flew by my ear as if teasing me. The green of the mountain ahead shimmered in the heat. Little by little I neared the shore.

Tug-of-War in the Moonlight

I am the same age as your grandmother Naomi. But I was better friends with her sister Machiko. I was born in Nishifure in Komaki and had an older sister named Yone, who has now passed away. She was the same age as Machiko. Machiko was pretty. I remember well going to watch the tug-of-war together.

Our tug of war event was known as Bon-tsuna because it was held around the Bon-festival. As the festival approached, we all gathered to make the rope. It was always held under the moonlight at the same place in Kurosaki. A few days before the festival, they started to beat drums to let people know that the event was to be held soon. Many people came from near and far. Everyone was part of one team or the other. It was so much fun that even my mother used to go.

I went with my sister and Machiko. She was probably fifteen years old then. She wore a pretty summer kimono, a Yukata. Men, seeing her, became giddy and started to show off. The Imanaga brothers from Kurosaki were particularly in high spirits that day. They were both fond of Machiko. They would do anything to try to impress her.

The oldest brother, Ryusuke, later became a member of the Yakuza. The second brother, Katsuji, did not quite reach that level, was restless but fun to be around. My sister was fond of Katsuji. She had been friends with the brothers since childhood. But both of them liked Machiko not her, she told me later.

The Imanaga brothers, Machiko, my sister, and myself often played together.

In summer we went to the sea. In the evening on the beach at low tide, Katuji made torches from bamboo and oil.

After dark if you walked along the beach with a torch in your hand, octopuses would follow you. We used to catch them to eat for dinner. Whenever Machiko tried to grab an octopus, Ryusuke took over saying "I'll get it for you." He was trying to impress her. But she would say, "I am not scared, not a bit." Even though she was from a well-to-do family, she could take care of herself.

Living by the sea, we did not have any rice field of our own or any woodland to collect wild herbs or mushrooms.

When we went to the beach, my sister would make rice balls for lunch. Her rice balls were made of wheat, not rice, mixed with sweet potatoes or in winter with millet. They were wrapped up in dried bamboo sheaths. Even our rice cakes were made from millet, not rice. When they became hard, we put them in water. So we called them water cakes. We thought Machiko would not eat such things because she was from a good family, but she ate them saying "Delicious." That made us happy. "I like her because of that," Ryusuke used to say.

Those are my fond memories.

Katsuji was good natured, but had the appearance of a gangster, not a real gangster, a self-proclaimed gangster. He even cut off his own left little finger. He had a tattoo, but it was incomplete. Because it was so painful and he did not have enough money, it was only half finished. It was a fearful looking tiger with its two hind legs missing. He liked to pretend that he was a bad guy, but that only made people laugh. My sister said that he did all this just to attract Machiko's attention. He should have known better. In the end Katsuji disappeared. He was such a fool. He was coaxed by someone on the mainland into becoming a loan shark. He lent a lot of money to people, but could not collect it back. So he got himself into deep trouble with the gangsters. He ended up fleeing the island. No one knows his whereabouts.

Ryusuke was warned by Yasutaro, Machiko's father and your great grandfather, never to see her again. My sister told me so. He left the island at an early age, and became a real yakuza on the mainland. When he occasionally returned, he wore a fine suit with an expensive looking watch. Unlike his younger brother, Ryusuke was a man of spirit. He became, not just any yakuza, but a high ranking member.

He killed someone in a gang-fight, and went on the run. It made the news. A rival gang came to the island searching for him, as his parents' house was still here. They hung around for some time and found out that he was likely to be in Shikoku. Later he was found and killed there.

The third Imanaga brother was a simple farmer. He was asked by the members of yakuza whether he wished to hold Ryusuke's funeral on the island. "No way!" He went to the mainland alone to attend the funeral. No other family member was present. It was held at his gang's headquarter. At the entrance of the funeral hall, lining up on the right side were all the members of the yakuza, and facing them on the left side were policemen. Walking between them, he felt his heart in his mouth. He felt a sense of dread at his own brother's funeral. As he was asked what to do about a grave, he replied, "There is no need to return the remains to the island." He was just an ordinary farmer, you know.

Machiko was not aware that both Ryusuke and Katsuji liked her. So my sister told me. My sister married a farmer, and I went to work at a shop dealing in Kimono fabrics. We lost contact with Machiko. After all she was from a different social standing and had problems of her own.

On reflection, Machiko had a big influence on me and my choice to work at the shop. Seeing her often wearing beautiful kimonos must have affected me. The shop I worked at still exists. The name of the shop was Nagata Kimono-store, but was known locally as 'Oyorimasse'. We used to say, "Let's go to Oyorimasse to buy a kimono." Because the shop staff shouted "Oyorimasse! Come-on-in! Oyorimasse! Come-on-in!" trying to coax passersby to enter. Well, in those days a cotton kimono was about four yen. When the war broke out, we all started to wear loose trousers.

I worked as a full-time live-in member of staff. The salary was four-yen a month. In addition I was given a roll of kimono fabric for the New Year, and another roll for the Bon Festival. Kimono fabric was normally sold by the roll, but in those days it was also sold by length, making us quite busy. When the war began, a fortress headquarter was set up just across from Eika Elementary school. You couldn't enter if you are civilian unless you had some kind of work connected with the fort. We had to show a stamped paper permission slip. I took various things there, such as bleached cotton cloth. I used to visit the army official residence with four or five rolls of kimono fabric, saying, "Would you like something?" or "This is a new arrival." Sometimes wives of army officials would give me some souvenirs saying they had been back home. It made me so happy, as what I received was better than anything you could find on the island.

I worked about fifteen years at the shop, then I got

married. One of our customers helped me to find a husband to be. "I am worried about you," he would say. "I know someone perfect for you." Actually he introduced me to one of his relatives.

My husband? Oh, I can't say that I was lucky. I didn't know he was an only son. He was spoiled and the apple of his parents' eye. My husband was a farmer, and he also worked for a construction company. He died of a stroke at seventy-eight. He drank too much, too much shochu.

Oh, sorry. I have talked too much about myself. As you say, I may be the only person alive who remembers Machiko when she was young. Until recently you could have spoken to Nari from the cask maker's, or Shige from the candy shop. But they have both passed away. Machiko was really pretty. She looked so wonderful that night in her summer kimono. The Bon-tsuna festival had a long history. Of course it had to be canceled during the war years, and unfortunately never took place again after that. How I miss it!

Knees

On the morning of my very first day of elementary school, I didn't let go of my sister's hand from the front door of our house to the school. I did not want to go into my own classroom alone, so I just followed my sister into her classroom. Looking back now I am surprised I could get away with this. Maybe it was because of the time we were living in or maybe it was because we were on a peaceful island. I am not sure. Her classroom teacher prepared a low chair for me. I was a pale and sickly child and seldom smiled. Only when I became a second grader, was I able to go to my own class. But I couldn't respond when I was spoken to, and it became an unspoken rule that they would treat me like a ghost. I gradually disappeared.

I felt no attachment to my home, either. Our house was called 'the Honke, the residence of the head of the family'. The house had belonged to my grandparents, but after my grandfather passed away, the five members of our family moved in. The house was surrounded by forest. Growling sounds could be heard on windy days as the leaves rustled and branches swayed. On the moonless nights the evil spirits residing in the forest would appear.

I had an older brother. There was quite an age difference between us. He would shut himself in his room as soon as he returned from school. He never played with me, or smiled at me. And I made no effort either, so we ended up acting like complete strangers to each other. My brother looked like my father. My father was the deputy mayor and always came home late. When we passed each other on the stairs at night, his face was always expressionless as if wearing a mask. There were three people wearing masks in our house; my father, my brother and me.

One hot and humid summer night, having difficulty in going to sleep, I decided to drink some barley tea. On my way to the kitchen, in the corridor, I looked into the living room for no particular reason, and saw my brother reading a book on the veranda. My father wearing his summer kimono approached him.

Looking down at his son he said, "Genzo, you are always reading useless books." My brother looked up at his father, said nothing, stood up and walked away through the living room towards the stairs. My father seemed to have no intention of continuing the conversation, and stood there looking out onto the garden. My brother saw me in the corridor, stopped and looked at me for a few seconds, and just continued up the stairs in silence.

He left the island as soon as he finished high school. He failed his university entrance examination, and started studying at a cram school in Fukuoka. But he did not seem to be very disappointed at all. On his occasional return, he would read books, the same way as he always did.

Every year, at the beginning of school, we had a physical strength and fitness test. In the fifth grade, just as every year, my test results were average. The last part of the test was a fifty-meter dash. We ran two at a time. My turn came, and I set off at the teacher's whistle.

While running, I felt the air rushing against my ears. I ran past the finish line, and just kept on running for a while. As I slowed down and turned back, I saw the other girl had just reached the finish line. The timekeeper was shouting something holding up her stopwatch, suddenly a great cheer arose.

I could not understand what was happening at first. Was it because I had grown a little taller? I looked down at my legs. Compared with other students' legs, mine might be slightly longer. Their legs were more or less curved, but mine were straight.

From that day on, people started talking about me being a fast runner. On my way to or from school, my neighbors would say to me, "We are counting on you in the relay." The elementary school sports day was held in autumn, and it was taken much more seriously than one would expect. The students and their families from each area of the village would compete against each other. Half of the programs were made up of events for the adults.

The rumor reached our family. My sister said leaning her head in wonder, "neither my brother nor I can run quickly." My mother couldn't, either. I did not know whether my father was fast or not. He had never come to our sports day. He was the only adult who did not show up.

I was chosen as a member of the inter-area relay race. Six pupils representing each grade of elementary school and four adults representing each generation, ten people in total passed the baton. We used to practice during the summer holiday. We used a red plastic baton. I liked the feel of it on my palm as it was passed to me. When I held it, I felt I could run even faster.

That year for the first time, my father came to watch. He sat beside my mother fanning himself.

We were well behind in third place. I overtook two

runners in front of me, and passed the baton on. The next runner, the sixth grader, and the remaining runners managed to hold onto our position in first place.

At the dinner table that evening, unusually, my father praised me. "You were great, Erika," he said sipping cold sake, "I am proud of you."

From that day, I no longer felt tense in the classroom. My stiff facial muscles were relaxed, and I was even able to manage an awkward smile.

In the sixth grade, I was again chosen as a relay member. We practiced baton passing at the school playing fields during summer holidays.

Just before the end of the holiday, my father suddenly passed away.

The cause of his death was a cerebral hemorrhage. At the funeral, people approached me and said, "Be strong."

On the sports day, I ran with all my might. While running everyone cheered me clapping their hands. I probably looked as if I was trying hard to overcome the sadness. Maybe I was, I am not sure. I do not really remember how I was feeling at that time.

I entered junior high school. As soon as the entrance ceremony was over, senior members of the girls' track and field club came to invite me to join them. I signed up as I was told. The adviser of the club was Mr. Yamada, a PE teacher. He had a crew cut and the hem of his shirt was tightly tucked into his jersey pants.

I touched a starting block for the first time at the club.

Mr. Yamada confessed that he would not be able to give any advice for the crouching start. He said that they did not have it when he was an active runner, and told us to think by ourselves and come up with a way that suited us the best.

Kawazoe, a second grader, was the best starter. Her start-dash was divinely beautiful. She kicked the air, then placed her foot on the block. She then straightened her knee and raised her neck. Raising her hips high, she set off as if released from a catapult. I tried to imitate her start-dash. I copied her as closely as possible, the way she flung her arms, the timing, and how she raised her upper body. She rotated her ankles while stretching her arms before taking her position. I even copied her idiosyncrasies. I ended up buying the same spikes as her.

During the summer holiday, we had a track and field tournament in which all the junior high schools on the island took part. There used to be as many as eleven schools, but now we only have four as a result of a decreasing population and government cut backs. On the morning of the tournament, Mr. Yamada handed out Hachimaki, headbands. They were black with the school name 'Hakozaki Junior High' embroidered on them in yellow.

"The day has come," he said.

At that time there was no nationwide athletic meet for junior high schools, so this tournament was actually as important as it got for us.

In the individual event I reached the finals. Kawazoe was in the next lane. We took our own position in the same posture, and sprinted in the same form. She came first, and I was second.

I also took part in the 400 meters relay. Kawazoe, the second runner, came into the relay zone in first place outpacing the other runners. I, as the third runner, carefully received the baton and keeping first place passed on the baton to the anchor.

The following day, the result of the tournament was reported on the front page of the local daily paper with pictures. The headline read 'Hakozaki Junior High Complete Victory', as the boys of our school also had good results. Lying on the floor, I looked at the picture in the center of the newspaper. It was a picture of us four relay members. I was smiling with my mouth open beside Kawazoe. As it was black and white picture, the whiteness of my teeth was unusually noticeable. I was now a suntanned healthy looking athletic girl. I raised myself and sat on the tatami with my legs stretched out. Brown thighs and shins. I somehow felt strange looking at myself.

The following year we won everything again. I was first in the individual hundred-meter dash. Kawazoe was second. She said "Congratulations" to me. In the relay I was entrusted with the position of the anchor. Kawazoe remained the second runner. Mr. Yamada placed his ace second. I broke the tape as our team won for the second consecutive year.

Kawazoe whispered in my ear after her graduation ceremony, "I will be waiting for you at the Commercial High School."

In the summer of my final year at junior high school, my brother came back the day before the tournament. By then he was a student of the department of economics at a private college in Fukuoka. He had his hair permed in a strange way. In an attempt to communicate with me, he said, "Fukuoka is a big city and really nice, you know." And "I've never won the first prize in anything." I did not know how to respond. My behavior towards him was still awkward but different from before. I was an adolescent girl, and although he was my own brother, he was still a male and older than me.

I took off my headband just before the finals of the hundred-meter dash. I looked at the embroidered letters 'Hakozaki Junior High', then tightly tied it around my head again. I adjusted the starting-block and tried it a few times to make sure it felt right. I saw my mother, my brother, and my sister in her office uniform near the finish line. My sister had finished high school that spring, and started working for a construction company on the island as an accountant. She came expressly to see me run, taking some time off work. Next to her, my brother was talking to my mother, and suddenly I understood why he had changed. It was not because he had left the island, nor that he had entered the college. He had grown up, become more responsible in order to take care of our mother.

"What made me think like this now of all time?" I slapped myself, stretched out my arms and loosened my ankles one by one.

"On your marks!"

I walked to my fourth lane starting position.

In the third lane was Matsuishi Chieko from Mushozu Junior High School, who was first in the other semi-final. And in the fifth lane was another good runner Nakanaga Junko, a third grader from Katsumoto Junior High School.

While gazing at the finish line, one hundred meters ahead, everything around me became silent and started moving in slow motion. My hands were in position. After kicking my foot in the air, I placed it on the block, stretched my elbows and raised my head.

"Ready!"

The voice of the starter sounded strangely clear.

I raised my hips, and posed.

The signal gun fired. The moment the sound reached my eardrums my reflexes took over, and my body reacted. I raised my upper body and started to sprint. I felt a gust of wind at my back. The last twenty meters. The last ten meters. I did not slow down. There was no one in front of me.

I had passed the finish line before I knew it. I continued gradually slowing down until I reached walking pace, and then I turned around. I was first. It was my personal best and a new record for the event.

Nakanaga Junko was second, and Matsuishi Chieko third. I looked down at my legs. They seemed to have a life of their own. In the final of the relay my legs moved unbelievably well too. After receiving the baton from the third runner in fourth place, I overtook three runners and finished first.

As I was preparing to go home after the award-giving ceremony, Matsuishi Chieko and Nakanaga Junko approached me. It was the first time I had ever talked with them, but Nakanaga spoke to me as if we had been friends for some time, "You are so fast." She asked me which high school I would go to the following year. There were two high schools on the island; a general high school and a commercial high school. I replied without much thinking, "To the Commercial

High School." Then she said, "Then I will go there, too." I was dumbfounded. Then Matsuishi said, "That's where I'm going, too."

The headline of the following day's paper read "Golden age of Hakozaki Junior High," and reported in detail that our relay team had won for three consecutive years, and that I had set a new record. In retrospect, it was certainly my golden age.

In February my sister married her childhood friend. He worked for a company in Kitakyushu. So, I lived alone with my mother at home. I felt that the wooden floor had become colder and the rooms a little darker.

But I had my running. On the first day at high school, I went to the teachers' room to hand in an application for the track and field club. The coach of the club was Mr. Jimbo who was said to have some experience of coaching on the mainland.

He was a young teacher of about thirty and he wore a light blue jersey top and matching sweat pants.

"I was so happy when I learned that you three were coming to our school."

Matsuishi Chieko and Nakanaga Junko were standing beside me. Nakanaga called me 'Eri'. So I called her 'Jun'. Naturally Matsuishi was called 'Chie'.

After practicing together for a few weeks, I became aware of the others' natural ability. Kawazoe was the best in the school, and Aida, a third grader, was the next best. We three were probably faster than any other older students.

The Prefectural Track and Field Meeting was scheduled

for the final weekend of June. It would be our first big official meeting. If we did well, we would qualify for the all Kyushu event, the next step after that would be the all Japan finals. The Nationwide High School Track and Field Meeting was set up soon after the Second World War. It was said that high school club activities were intended to help students better themselves. I first began to realize this when I started high school.

The Commercial High School was on the far side of the island, which meant I had to take a bus. It would take me two hours one way from my house to the school, and it would affect my practice in the club. My cousin Tetsuro offered to give me a ride. He was the same age as me and went to the other high school. He was the only student who went to school by car.

"My mother bought it for me," he said unconcernedly.

The car ran at full speed on the empty country road, leaving clouds of dust in its wake. "I feel bad for keeping you waiting until my practice finishes."

Turning the steering wheel, Tetsuro shook his head.

"Don't worry. In fact it gives me a good excuse as I can enjoy myself in Gonoura."

At first I thought he said this so that I didn't need to worry. But he actually was having fun in Gonoura which was the busiest town on the island. He picked me up on his way back.

At the end of May, Mr Jimbo announced the 400 meters relay team members. None of us first graders were included. I wondered why. Amongst the second and third graders only Kawazoe and Aida were faster than us. On the same day, kit for the events was handed out. White running shirts and black running pants with a white stripe down the side. I felt happy because they made me feel like an Olympic athlete. The Prefectural Meeting was held at the Prefectural Athletic Stadium in Nagasaki City. We were badly beaten in both the individual and relay events. I was only a frog in the well, and I realized that there were lots of people who could run faster than me.

In those days my mother frequently went to Fukuoka to see my brother. It worried me as she seemed to me to be much too dependent on him. But I was busy enough with my own affairs. Although I had been practicing hard, I could not better the time I had made in junior high school. I was struggling, and continued to struggle until, suddenly, a year had gone by. The time had come again for the Prefectural Track and Field Meeting.

Although we did not do well in the individual events, all three of us, Jun, Chie and myself, were chosen as 400 meters relay members. The first runner was Jun, I was second, Chie third and the anchor Kawazoe. This team was fast. We easily got through the preliminary heat. In the final Kawazoe did her best and we finished in third place in a close race. And we qualified to advance to the All Kyushu Meeting.

It was held at Heiwadai Track and Field Stadium in Fukuoka City. The stands were so large that it made me feel as if I were at the Tokyo Olympic Stadium. My heart beat with excitement. My mother and my brother came to watch. My brother had graduated from university that spring and had started working for a company in Fukuoka. It was drizzling that day, and the track was not in great condition, but we roused ourselves to get through to the semi-finals and just managed to advance to the finals.

The 400 meters relay final. If we finished in the top six, we would qualify for the Nationwide Meeting. I became so nervous. I tried to calm myself by jumping up and down.

"On your marks!"

We were in the second lane. Jun placed her foot on the starting block. I could hear my heart beat. Before I realized it everything became silent.

"Ready!"

The starter held his pistol high in the air.

Finally, the moment had come. The starting gun fired. Jun took off. She rounded the corner. She was coming closer. I started to run holding out my right arm behind me. I felt the baton on my palm. I held it firmly and accelerated leaning forward. When I raised my upper body, out of the corner of my eye, I saw six other runners in front of me. I felt the wind on my back. My body was pushed forward. I overtook two. I saw Chie and her right arm. I passed the baton. I shouted, "Go, Chie! Go!"

Chie skillfully rounded her corner. Kawazoe started to run. The baton was passed, but the timing was slightly off. Kawazoe had to pause for an instant, and she was overtaken by two runners. She could not catch up, and finished in seventh place.

We had not qualified. I suddenly felt weak, and found it difficult to stay on my feet, so I crouched down.

We had come so close. Then I managed to stand up and look around, noticing that something was going on. The referees had gathered in front of the official tent and were discussing something. Everyone was watching them with bated breath. Shortly one of the referees went up onto the platform with a loudspeaker.

"There was a violation of the rules by Honryo High School from Oita prefecture in the sixth lane. They had overran when passing the baton from the third runner to the fourth. Therefore Honryo High School has been disqualified. Everyone behind them will move up a place."

I immediately started to run to Kawazoe who was still near the finish line. Both Jun and Chie came running. "We've qualified, we've qualified!" Tears streamed down our faces.

That year the Nationwide Track and Field Meeting was to be held in Hiroshima in the first week of August. "Off to Hiroshima!" read the local paper. The whole island was excited. We received generous amount of sea bream and rice as gifts of encouragement. We had three weeks to prepare. Mr. Jimbo reduced our practice schedule for fear of exhaustion. I felt we needed to work harder but we followed his advice.

Ten days before the meeting, Tetsuro showed up when we were practicing. He whispered something to our coach. Mr. Jimbo called me over.

"Change and go home," was all he said. Tetsuro looked unusually quiet.

His car was parked just outside the school gate. As soon as I sat down next to him, he said, "Well, let's go." And he started his car, and drove silently looking straight ahead.

"Has something happened?"

"It's Genzo."

"My brother? What has he done?"

Tetsuro stopped the car in the middle of the road.

"They are saying that he has had a motorbike accident."

I felt faint all over. The blood drained from my body.

"Is he injured?"

He accelerated ignoring my question. From then until we reached home, he remained silent. Unexpectedly I found my uncle and my aunt already there. My mother was crying and unconsolable. My brother had been killed in an accident at a junction in Fukuoka, so I was told.

The last thing I felt like doing was running. I told Mr. Jimbo that I would not be going to Hiroshima. He nodded and said, "Be strong." I was replaced by a younger student.

Four days before the meeting, all the relay team members came to see me.

Chie had tears in her eyes.

"Eri, come on, let's run together!"

"I'm sorry," was all I could say.

Kawazoe held my shoulder, and said, "Be strong."

I nodded, but inwardly said to myself, "No, I can't. I can't be strong!"

My sister stayed with us for some time before returning to Kitakyushu. My mother was beside herself. I seriously feared that she might go mad. So I took over all the housework. There was so much to do. After the Nationwide Meeting, Kawazoe came to report that they had lost in a preliminary heat.

When the second term started, I declined Tetsuro's kind

offer of a lift, and started taking the bus to school. I also left the club. After being away from practice for a while, I could not see the meaning of running. You started, you finished and someone timed how long it took. For that, I had sacrificed my time, my energy.

I have no recollection of school life after that.

After finishing high school, I went to Osaka to work and got a job in the accounting division in a dress making company. I decided to leave the island because I feared staying in that gloomy house would spoil my life. I had an easy life in Osaka, but that was all. After working for a year, I thought I had had enough and perhaps I would find a job on the island. Upon returning, I found my mother had not recovered yet. She always carried a tin car about with her. It was a blue car, a childhood treasure of my brother. It was sad to see and at the same time it scared me a little.

I could not find a good job on the island, and had to go to Fukuoka to work, after all. At first, I worked as a telephone operator at Fukuoka Airport. Watching airplanes flying off every day, it never occurred to me that I wanted to go somewhere. I worked there for two years, and left for no particular reason. After that I found an accounting job in a company in the city. I worked there for forty years. I did have a few boyfriends, but in the end I remained single.

My mother passed away seven years ago. When she was still alive, she did not need me. What she needed was my brother. She kept thinking of her dead son. I am not saying this out of resentment, or jealousy. I am simply stating a fact.

This spring I reached my retirement age, and had no

desire to return to the island. During the first month after retirement I just stayed home doing nothing. Then somehow my knees started to ache. The pain became worse and worse, and in the end I could hardly walk. I visited an orthopedics department. The doctor told me it was osteoarthritis. Back home sitting on a dining chair, I looked down at my knees and thought that I would not be able to run again, suddenly I became sad. I have not done any sport since I stopped running at the second year of high school. Frequent visits to the doctor made my knees feel better.

The other day, I was invited to join a local senior citizens club. To be sixty-five is considered to be old aged. I was told it was going to be some kind of a tea party, but actually it was more like an office meeting. They even had a white-board. The subject we discussed that day was the upcoming senior citizens sports day. They said that it was an annual event and everyone took it quite seriously.

"As you are still young, you must take part in a relay race." I was concerned about my knees, but thought it would be all right as long as I was careful not to overdo it.

"I want to run the second leg," I said.

"No. A young one like you should be the anchor."

"Please, let me run the second leg," I insisted ignoring their odd looks.

Fifty years had passed since that summer.

Gessekai

The memorial service of the fiftieth anniversary of Genzo's death was held at Kogenji-temple in Honmura-hamlet. After the service, we all split into different groups and headed for the Hirayama Inn by car. Mr. Kunimura, a friend of the deceased, was the only attendee other than the relatives. He was from Sangenjaya, the same town as Genzo. He left the island when he was young and became a school teacher in Fukuoka. He settled there and stayed on even after his retirement. At the dinner we sat facing each other. He had good posture for his age, and looked youthful and healthy. He gave the impression of being a clean cut decent man, and I noticed his suit and shirt had no wrinkles.

Usually at memorial services dinner is simple and vegetable based, however on this occasion on the table was a real feast including sea bream sashimi and lobster tempura.

Yoshiko, Genzo's sister, had brought an album with a collection of Genzo's pictures. Passing around the album, we talked about old times. The first page showed a photograph seemingly of his elementary school graduation ceremony. The next page was Genzo in school uniform standing to attention in front of his front door. There were thirty to forty pictures in total arranged in chronological order, one of which was Genzo posing Ivy League style holding a guitar. My aunt said turning the pages, "There aren't many pictures of him smiling, are there?" "Didn't Genzo smile much?" I asked Mr. Kunimura. With a taut face he replied, "Well, I'm not sure."

The last picture was a group photo taken at Genzo's funeral. Taking a group photo at a funeral seemed strange to me but maybe it was not so in those days. Naturally Genzo was not in the photo. As I held it my uncle sitting beside me glanced at it and pointed asking, "Who is this woman?" She was standing at the far right of the back row and was the only one looking away from the camera.

The photo album was passed around again. Everyone wondered who she was, but nobody knew. The album was passed on to me again. I was not born yet when the photo was taken, so I did not recognize her or almost anyone in the picture. I showed the picture to Mr. Kunimura and asked, "Don't you know her?" Staring at it, he said, "No, I don't." I got the impression he was lying. I handed him my business card, and told him that I had been researching my family history and the island.

Two months later, I received mail from Mr. Kunimura. Five sheets of letter paper were folded in the envelope.

*

Dear Sir,

Thank you very much for inviting me to the memorial service of the fiftieth anniversary of Genzo's death. At the dinner I enjoyed looking at the pictures which brought back fond memories of his life and those days. I felt fifty years of time rewind in an instant.

Honestly, I have been in two minds about whether to write this letter or not. However I came to the conclusion that what I have to say will not hurt anyone since already half a century has passed, and, from a personal point of view, it will give me some peace of mind. However writing about the past means disclosing my own love affairs, which of course is embarrassing, and that is the reason it took me so long to make up my mind. It seems even my introduction is rather long.

At the dinner, you asked me two questions. One was whether Genzo smiled or not, and the other was about the young woman in the group photo at his funeral. My answer to both questions at the time was 'I don't know.' However, as you may have guessed, this is not strictly true.

When we were at elementary school, Genzo and I used to play together with neighboring children until dark every day, running about the fields and forests, or diving into the river. I noticed at quite an early stage that Genzo did not laugh heartily or show any real signs of joy, but I never mentioned it. I was not the kind of child who was good at expressing his thought.

There always seemed to be something bothering Genzo. Probably his parents were partly to blame for his dark disposition. In fact, some years later when he was completely drunk, he told me so himself. Even though the next day he probably forgot everything he said. His parents did not get along with each other, their relationship was somewhat distant and lacked warmth, though they did not reveal this in public.

Genzo thought that the complications and discord between his parents was caused by their inferiority complex towards your grandfather and grandmother. As you know, his father Sadakichi, the head of the main family, was the deputy mayor, whereas his brother-in-law, that is your grandfather Hiroki, the head of a branch family, was a doctor. It was your grandfather who succeeded the medical profession of the late head of the family. Sadakichi and his wife must have felt their headship was taken away from them, this eventually affected their relationship. Genzo had assimilated all their difficulties.

It may be unthinkable in modern society, but at that time the headship of the family involved an unreasonable amount of responsibility and importance. It could be oppressive and in some cases life changing. Home could be a restrictive and uncomfortable place. Have people forgotten such an oppressive atmosphere existed? It seems to me people today are apt to romanticize the old days. But the old days were never better than now.

Genzo became introverted around the time he entered junior high school and he would spend most of the time alone reading books. He left the island as soon as he finished high school, and started to study at a cram school in Fukuoka. I think it was your father's influence. Your father and Genzo were cousins of similar age who seemed to get on well despite of their parents' differences. At least your father did not seem to give much importance to such things. But I am not sure what Genzo really thought.

Your father, during his time as a student at a cram school, was a bandsman at a cabaret in Nakasu. It was the heyday of cabarets and there were so many of them in that area. He played the sax at the cabaret 'Gessekai' in Nishi-Nakasu. Jazz music was very popular. Glen Mirror, Duke Elington were played by big bands at all of the cabarets. His exploits must be the reason your father had to repeat cram school several times before he successfully entered university.

Through an introduction by your father, Genzo also started to work at Gessekai as an apprentice, and he started practicing Jazz-guitar around that time. He became part of the night life scene. He might have been a lazy student, but he certainly came to life at night.

After some years at cram school, he finally managed to enter Fukuoka University. In the same year his father Sadakichi suddenly passed away with a cerebral hemorrhage. We used to see each other quite often. I was studying mathematics at Kyushu University. Losing his father seemed to sap some of the life out of him. He did his best to appear cheerful in front of his mother when she visited him. When she was not around, he appeared soulless.

Even so he did not leave Nakasu. He continued to practice the guitar, but he was not considered good enough to become a bandsman. He became intimate with a hostess at Gessekai, and soon started acting like her pimp. The name of the hostess was Nomiyama Saeko. She used the working name Lily at Gessekai. She is the girl in the photo.

Their relationship continued up until the day of his fatal accident. I sometimes spent time together with them, having dinner or going to the cinema. I believe your father went out with them too. He probably does not remember her because he left Fukuoka to enter Kurume Medical School. Genzo's mother, Machiko, seemed to be aware of her existence, and of course was not very happy about it. Genzo never introduced her to his mother.

She was so pleased for him when he finally graduated from university and started to work for a trading company. She continued to work at the cabaret, but sometimes they spoke of getting married. It must have taken a lot of courage for her to attend his funeral. Even so she wanted to say a final farewell to him. I think she really loved him.

I, too, was so shocked by his death. I realized how transient a life could be. He had a very difficult childhood and adolescence but his adult life was just about to begin. All that was lost in an instant.

As his friend, I was trying to comfort her. What I am ashamed about and find difficult to tell you is that we too became intimate. At the time, I worked as a teacher at a public school in Fukuoka City, and she continued to work as a hostess at Gessekai. Our relationship continued for nearly two years. In fact I even proposed to her. She laughed and did not take me seriously.

What I am going to tell you now may be too personal and specific. The second summer after we started dating, we went to Unzen Spa to spend the weekend. I happened to wake up in the middle of night. I sat up and looked towards the window, and saw Saeko sitting there. As I approached her, she looked up at me. I noticed there was a beer bottle and for some reason two glasses on the table. One from which Saeko had already drunk and the other filled up to the rim.

She was probably offering Genzo a glass of beer. I said nothing, and Saeko also remained silent. For some time after that we both acted as if nothing had happened. But soon I could bear it no more. When I come to think of it now, I cannot believe why I did not try harder to understand her feelings. I was such a narrow-minded man. "Let's separate," I said. Saeko nodded and did not even ask why. The cabaret 'Gessekai' closed a few years after that. I do not know what became of her. I married the woman my parents had arranged for me, and was blessed with three children. My wife passed away three years ago with liver cancer. This may be a commonplace expression, but although Genzo died young, he has always been alive in me. In other words, I feel that somewhere in me I have always lived with his death.

I hope this provides you with some answers. I accept my sense of disgrace but feel that these memories form part of both mine, Genzo and Saeko's past. I hope you can find some meaning or worth in all this.

Please take care of yourself.

Yours sincerely,

Kakizome

- The First Calligraphy of the New Year

I am a repatriate. My three sisters and I were all born in Taiwan.

I was born in the countryside of Tainan Province and later moved to the center of Tainan City. My father worked at the police pharmacy there. The local workers at the pharmacy were very kind to us. Do you know a kind of citrus fruit called Bontan? They used to give us things like that. We used to share them with our neighbors. We lived in the official police residence in Nanmon-cho. It was a quite large one-story house with four rooms. Higashi-Ichiba market was nearby.

At that time in Taiwan, there were two types of elementary schools, Japanese and Taiwanese. In Tainan there were two Japanese elementary schools, Nanmon and Hanazono. I used to go to Nanmon elementary school. It took me about twenty minutes on foot to get there. It was near Tainan Shrine. We wore uniforms that looked like sailor suits both for winter and summer.

The other school was only for Taiwanese children. However, the children of wealthy families often attended the Japanese schools. There were one or two Taiwanese children in each class. Each grade had four classes, two for girls and two for boys.

Saeki, one of my classmates, lived in an official residence near ours. She now lives in Kumamoto. We used to play a lot together, skipping, hopscotch, making rope with rubber bands, and playing with beanbags.

Calligraphy was very important at our school. Hanazono was better known for art, painting and drawing. We had two calligraphy teachers. My teacher was Mr. Okadome. He was from Kagoshima. He had a long beard and looked like a hermit. There was a calligraphy contest once a year for all elementary schools in Taiwan. I won the first prize when I was in the second grade. I wrote "日の丸" Hinomaru, the rising sun.

We had a Taiwanese girl in my class. She got the second prize. Her name was Mou Kyoka, but to enter Japanese school at that time she had to change her name to Mouri Kyoko. The school was so proud of having two children from the same class win first and second prize.

Mouri was a tall, fair-skinned pretty girl. Most girls had their hair bobbed, but hers was dark and very long. She was smart, too. She didn't talk much, but when she did, it was clear and concise.

She took different after-school lessons including a piano lesson almost every day, and didn't have many friends. I was one of her few good friends. I visited her house several times. Her father owned a toy company and was very rich. They lived in a big house with a landscaped garden. In the house there were a lot of toys made of wood. As I went up the stairs, each step made the sound of the musical scale, do, re, mi, fa, so⋯. I was surprised. I wondered where the sound came from. (Some kind of toy-like device must have been installed.)

The late Emperor, the Showa Emperor, visited Taiwan when he was still a prince. It was before I was born. As part of his official tour he visited our school. The school held a festival commemorating that particular day; April 20th. One year, I was chosen together with Mouri to sing a song on the assembly hall stage.

During the New Year, Donto-yaki was held at the school. First a tower was made, then a fire was lit. You put your Kakizome paper on one end of a bamboo stick and held it to the fire. The paper would float into the sky because of the heat. They used to say that the higher up the paper went, the better you would be at calligraphy. Both Mouri's and my piece of paper went quite high. It was fun. After that we gathered in the hall. As we gazed at the stage, the curtain was raised, and the Emperor's portrait appeared.

When I was in the fourth grade, our grandfather who lived in Tanie on Iki-island fell ill. It being war time, my father had been moved to the front in Hainan-island to support the army. So my mother, my sister and I returned to the island to visit our grandfather. We stayed there for a month. As it was quite a long time, I attended school on the island.

It was early Autumn, sports day season in Japan. I was invited to dance at the sports day. I had learned how to dance in Tainan. So our teacher told the students, "Every one, try to follow Kishi." The teacher was Ms. Baba. She was from Sasebo. Her son was studying in Tainan Technical School, so she was very kind to me when she learned that I was from Tainan.

Taiwan seemed to be very advanced when compared to Iki-island. We studied using notebooks in Taiwan, but on the island they used only pieces of paper. They didn't even have pencils and pencil cases. On the island rice was mixed with wheat. But in Tainan we had real Japanese rice. Even the way they spoke was so different. In Taiwan we used standard Japanese but they had a very strong dialect.

Returning to Taiwan, we first had to take a passenger boat

to Fukuoka. Everyone in my class came to see me off. I was surprised when Ms. Baba came running to me and gave me a big hug. From Fukuoka we took another ship to Taiwan. A ship which left a few days after ours was sunk and destroyed by a torpedo. We were lucky. After that the war escalated.

Shortly after we returned to Taiwan, there was a calligraphy contest. It was not just for Taiwan, but all East Asian countries including China and Japan. As it was during the war, I wrote '上げよ勝鬨', call to victory. I won the bronze prize.

I remember seeing Mouri handing her calligraphy to the teacher. She was sitting diagonally behind me. As I turned around, she stood up and went to the front holding her paper. I caught a glimpse of it. I could not see what she had written, but I managed to see her name. She had written "Mou Kyoka", not "Mouri Kyoko". Mr. Okadome took the paper with a stern look on his face, said nothing. Mouri didn't win a prize.

My father returned safely from the war. It was at this point that he was offered a job by a medical company in Taipei, so he quit his job at the police, and we all moved as a family. It was in December of the sixth grade. Our graduation was only three months away, but sadly I was unable to attend it with my classmates. We took the train from Tainan Station. Saeki, Mouri and some classmates took the day off school to see me off. We were all in tears. Mouri said with a deep sincerity, "Keep well." The tears that fell from her eyes were as straight as her calligraphy stroke.

Taipei came under heavy attack just before the end of the war and kept burning for many days. I don't remember any of my Taipei school friends well. As the war got worse, all we did at school was cut sheets of mica to be used to make radars.

One day while I was at school, my mother was at home busy looking after my new born sister. My other sister Natsuko, eight years younger than me, was playing with an oil drum next to our veranda. She sat astride the drum and hit it with a metal stick. Somehow she must have hit something else, perhaps a stray bullet. There was an explosion.

Our aunt was at that time working as a nurse at Japan Red Cross Hospital, and she took Natsuko there immediately. She survived, she was operated on, but lost her hand. She was five years old then. She was the only victim of war in my family.

The war ended when I was in the first year of Girl's school, and we returned to Japan. It was March of 1946. My youngest sister had her first birthday on the ship. She now lives in Osaka.

We took a repatriation ship from a port town called Kieloon, near Taipei. It was a cargo ship. All we were allowed to carry was the rucksack on our back. So I could only take a few pieces of clothing. We had to leave everything behind even the amount of money we could take was limited. Our ship sailed nonstop until it arrived at Tanabe in Wakayama-prefecture.

From there we took a train to Fukuoka, then a boat to the island. The boat Isao-maru was so small that I suffered from sea-sickness. It took nearly six hours.

When we returned to the island, I entered the second grade of Girl's school at what is now known as Mushozu Junior High School in Gonoura. I was a boarder. Five or six students shared one room. Each grade had two classes, Class A and Class B. I joined the school basketball club. We played on an outside court.

After finishing Girl's school, I started working at my uncle's clinic. He is your great grandfather, Yasutaro. I wanted to study more, but I had to work. My work involved wrapping medicine and all sorts of other things. His wife Kie was very strict. There was a man in Esumi, who was a little crazy in the head. When he passed by the clinic, he would start singing in a loud voice, "She is so beautiful but she is so cruel. That's our Kie!" It was so funny that we used to laugh under our breath.

I left the job at twenty-three and got married. My uncle gave me some furniture as a wedding present. My husband was a distant relative. His mother and my father were cousins. He had quite a good reputation. He was chosen for me by my uncle. I had never met him before. He was a farmer and seven years older than I. He also started working as a meter reader for Kyushu Electric Company. So I helped him with his work in the field and collecting electricity bills.

For some years, I did not know where all those students from Nanmon Elementary School ended up. But we had our first reunion in Fukuoka fifteen years after we returned from Taiwan. It was held at a hotel in front of Hakata Station. People came from all over Japan. I was able to meet Saeki who was my classmate and next-door neighbor. We still exchange letters. I have never heard from or about Mouri. I wonder if she is still alive.

There have been many reunions held in Tokyo or in Fukuoka since then, but I have only been able to attend

Fukuoka a few times, Tokyo is too far. I'm also still invited to the elementary school reunions here, even though I attended the school for only a month. Thanks to the reunions, I have many friends.

I have never been back to Taiwan. I wanted to go, but work and other things have prevented me. I have some friends from those days who now live in Fukuoka, Kumamoto and elsewhere. Some of them have returned to Taiwan many times. My sister has visited there too. She said that Taiwan had changed so much, but the official residence where we lived was still there. She is seven years older than me and used to work in a bank in Taiwan. She was very good with an abacus. When she came back to the island, our uncle, Yasutaro helped her to get a job at a local branch of the Japan Agricultural Cooperative. It used to be called 'Nokyo-kai'.

I have five children, all boys. Ironically I myself had only sisters. Raising my sons was trouble free and even now I have no worries from them. The first-born son took over his father's farm work. All of them have married and have their own houses.

I have lived alone since my husband passed away. I still enjoy calligraphy. I use your grandfather Hiroki's calligraphy as my reference point. His work was given to me when he was still alive. Every year there is a festival on the cultural day, November 3. I send my calligraphy to the exhibition held as a part of the cultural events at the Island Center. Last year I wrote "月到千家静", meaning the harvest moon is shining above thousands of houses making a serene atmosphere.

What shall I write this year?

The Balloon

I advanced thrusting my way through deep snow using my arms to help me as if swimming. Everything as far as I could see was covered with snow. Alone, I moved deeper into the forest.

This was the image that sprang to mind, when I was asked the question, "What is your first memory?" Obviously I am mistaken. This memory comes from the time I was recuperating in a sanatorium. I was in the North Ward for women, I was nineteen years old and it was winter. I should be able to remember much farther back.

I closed my eyes and thought a little harder. The next image that appeared in my mind was of a bear fur rug in the living room of my grandfather's house. The house was surrounded by the rice paddies and fields, but I had never seen my grandparents planting rice or plowing fields. My grandfather was probably a land owner or something like that. He was sitting cross-legged on the bear fur rug. He had a fine moustache like General Nogi. A photograph of my deceased father hung in the living room. My brother who was then three or four years old was looking up at the photograph. My brother was three years younger than me, so I must have been six or seven years old.

My father died when I was three.

At my father's funeral, my mother was weeping. One of my relatives was holding my baby brother.

"My first memory is a coffin, my father's coffin."

The man who posed the question seemed taken aback and lost for words.

My father who rebelled against his father worked in the accounting division of a small transport company. On the day of his death, they had the job of removing the safe from a bankrupt house. As there was not enough manpower, some people from the accounting division were asked for help. They were trying to bring down the safe from the mezzanine floor using a ladder. As my father voluntarily climbed up the ladder to grab the safe, the ladder broke. He fell and was crushed as the safe fell on top of him.

My grandfather said to my widowed mother, "I will raise the children, so you may return to your parents' house."

My mother refused and instead she decided to bring us up by herself.

I was born in a small country town called Honjo near Akita-city. The town now is thriving but in those days there were apple and pear orchards lining the mountain side. My mother worked as a tenant farmer during the day, and in the evening she earned extra money by making kimonos until late.

The year I entered elementary school, the pacific war broke out. As the war escalated, we were forced to dig up the roots of pine trees in the mountain instead of taking lessons. The pine trees had already been felled and only their roots were left. Removing the endless roots was children's work. After they were removed, bungalows were built. It was said that they were going to be used as the military sanatorium for tuberculosis.

Around the time I entered junior high school, I started to enjoy being alone. I loved to read books. I am not sure if I liked books because I was alone, or I liked being along because I liked books. That is not to say I did not have any friends. Hamaguchi Yumiko was a good friend of mine. She was the daughter of the sewing machine shop's owner and lived in a fine new house. There were many books in their study. I remember well the first book I borrowed from her. It was The Good Earth by Pearl Buck. Although it was in three volumes, I finished reading them in an instant. After that I frequently visited Hamaguchi's house to borrow some books.

I went to a girls' high school. While my classmates were enjoying chatting about boys from other schools, I read. My favorite book was The Red and the Black by Stendhal. However, I could not relate to what was happening between the men and the women in the book. It seemed unrealistic, distant, nothing to do with me.

In the winter of my last year at high school, I fell ill. After graduation, because of my condition, I found myself spending most of my time resting at home. I started to cough. I went to the doctor and was diagnosed with tuberculosis, and was told that I had to be hospitalized immediately. Ironically I was taken to the sanatorium built on the land where we had dug out the pine-tree roots when we were at elementary school. After the war they accepted not only disabled veterans but also general tuberculosis cases. It was a large open space filled with rows of one-story houses. My room was in the North Ward for women. It was for serious cases and had three patients in each room. I lay in my bed in distress. I was full of appreciation for my mother who had raised us up all by herself. And just as I was thinking it was time to show her my gratitude, I was hospitalized. It placed an unbearable strain on me.

One winter morning, I woke up and was making my bed as usual when one of my roommates returned from the washroom. "Good morning," we greeted each other. I went to wash my face and then to the toilet. When I returned to the room, I found the girl whom I had just spoken to had been coughing up blood. She was lying on the floor motionless. She was already dead.

I was relatively calm when it happened, but after three days I became suddenly overwhelmed by sadness. I slipped out of the sanatorium and wandered about in the coppice behind it. After walking aimlessly, I came to a point where the trees became more and more sparse and I was confronted by an open space covered with snow. I advanced farther struggling to force my way through the snow. Suddenly, I stopped and began to cry. After a while, I realized I was freezing cold. I dried my tears and returned.

I often sneaked out and walked around in the woods. Just beyond them was a river. I often read books sitting on the river bank. The sanatorium had a library with quite a good collection. The Magic Mountain by Thomas Mann. I could not stop turning the pages.

During the second spring of my hospitalization, the doctor in charge said to me, "It is time to operate." He explained about the operation by drawing pictures on a piece of paper. His plan was to operate on two occasions. He would first remove the right upper lobe of my lungs. The second step would be to remove some ribs. The first operation was a success, and I was moved to the South Ward. This ward was for more mild cases, but even so I felt depressed. I had good reason to be worried about the second operation. The chances were I would not live much longer after having my bones removed. My concern was real. In those days in order to fill the space where the tissue had been taken, an artificial pneumothorax was used. The patients used to call it 'the glass ball'. This space filling device could become a problem in itself. Eventually it had to be taken out. Many patients died during the removal operation. People who had been actively walking about the ward until the previous day, left the surgery as corpses. That was the reality I was faced with. I was expected to live no more than two or three years after the operation. I looked out of the window absentmindedly. I felt nothing as I stared at the flowers in the courtyard.

A month after the first operation, I was called to the doctor's room. I opened the door nervously. He handed me a paper bag. I saw lots of rubber balloons in it. "Try blowing into them, it may help your lungs." Then he said, "I won't be long," and left the room. I put one of them in my mouth. It expanded easily. It was fun. I repeated. When he returned, the room was filled with the balloons. He told me off, "You should know your limit," but nodded with a smile.

Blowing up the balloons may have helped. I did not have to have the second operation. Somewhere in my memory is the image of all sorts of multicolored balloons floating up to the ceiling of the doctor's room. Of course in reality this never happened as the balloons would have fallen softly to the floor.

A year after the operation I was given the all clear, and permission to leave the sanatorium. I had been completely cured.

I found a job at the Telephone Company as a typist. After working there for eight years, and when I was thirty, I decided to go to Tokyo. My brother who had married a few years before stayed at home. I told my mother it was quite difficult to live with my brother's family. But actually, my time in a sanatorium had had an effect on me. When I had my lung removed at the age of twenty-one, I didn't really expect to live this long. I wanted to give myself the chance to live as full a life as possible. A relative of mine who lived in Tokyo found me a bedsit and a job at a petrol station. I did not go to Tokyo to live an exciting life. I had no expectation of going out to drink in Ginza, or having a parfait at Shiseido Parlour.

I lived a modest life but it was dreamlike compared to what it might have been if I had stayed at home. I could drop by a secondhand bookstore on the way home after work, and read as much as I liked without feeling guilty.

I had almost no friends, nor did I want any. But I became acquainted with an older woman who lived next door. Her name was Takanashi Kimiko. I felt envious about her surname Takanashi, because it seemed to me a quite cosmopolitan name. She showed interest in the books on the shelf in my room. She was a proofreader of popular novels at the time. She had short hair, considered to be fashionable and was a modern girl, quite the opposite of myself who had just arrived from the country. The only thing we had in common was that we both had almost no other friends. We often visited each other's room taking snacks or cakes and having tea. We also went to a public bath together. She seemed to be always busy. Sometimes she allocated me some of her work. It was a good side business for me. The extra money enabled me to buy the complete series of a set of world literature. Guy de Maupassant, Hermann Hesse, and John Steinbeck. I was so happy having them in my room, and I read and reread them over and over again.

On the other hand I was quite concerned about my job. Working at the petrol station was quite tough on me. I saw an advertisement for a job at a timber import company in the newspaper, and I sent them my C.V. and was employed immediately. It was in Yokohama and had an office on the second floor of a western style building, overlooking the port. My job was to calculate the volume of imported building timber. I used a special chart to calculate the volume in cubic meters.

I rented a room in an apartment five minutes-walk from the office. Yokohama was more exotic than Tokyo, and I preferred it. After moving to Yokohama, I never went to visit Takanashi. It seems quite heartless when I come to think of it now. After all it was not very far by train.

One day, when I was thirty-two, an elderly obliging woman who lived near the office brought me an offer of marriage. She was going to introduce me to a boatman working on a barge. In those days a small boat that carried goods from a big ship was called a barge. My type of man was good looking like Sada Keiji, the actor, but this man had the face of a fisherman from the south. I came to learn that he was actually from a fishing village. I didn't think I would marry him, but in the end I gave in to their persuasion. We had a daughter. We both worked, and although we were not rich, we had enough to get by.

Around the time when our daughter became three, my husband said we should return to his hometown because he had to look after his parents. So we decided to move to Iki-island.

Before leaving Yokohama, I went to see Takanashi. We arranged to meet at Tokyo Station, and went to a restaurant nearby. I told her that I used to read a lot while I was single even after moving to Yokohama, but I hardly read any more after getting married. Then she said, "I also gave up literature." She still worked for a publishing company but now did a different kind of job, not proofreading. She explained what she did, but I could not understand it at all. I asked her many questions until she found it tiresome, saying, "It's the kind of job that anyone can do."

As we were getting on a passenger ship at Hakata Port, I suddenly had a spell of dizziness. It was just an instant, so probably my husband did not notice. I asked myself, "What am I doing here?" I was heading for a small island in the corner of Kyushu, far away from my hometown.

I had been told we were returning to the island to look after my parents-in-law, but the real reason they wanted us here was to pay off their debt. All the money I possessed was taken by my mother-in-law. While making us to shoulder all their debts, she behaved so cruelly. My husband went to sea on a squid boat. He brought home squids, I sliced them open, dried them in the sun, and pressed them flat, and took them to the fisherman's association. Most of this money we earned was used for repayment of their debt. All the remaining was taken by my mother-in-law. I found it unreasonable and incomprehensible that I had to endure such poverty.

After some years, I became acquainted with the doctor's wife by a mere coincidence. She might have pitied me when she learned about my situation, and she employed me as a clerk at their office. My neighbors wondered why. Because she was known to be unsociable, and avoided as much as possible any contact with other people. She was somehow very kind to me. It was quite hard for me to work in the office and keep house at the same time, but because of the salary I received, I somehow managed to make ends meet. In order to survive I had to be a little shrewd, I opened a secret bank account. She helped me to take my driving license using office expenses.

I managed to marry off my daughter, I nursed my mother in Akita and attended her deathbed. By the time I reached sixty, I had paid off all the debt of my parents-in-law. Just when I was thinking our life would become easier, my husband collapsed from cerebral infarction. He lost the use of his legs because of a stroke. He was hospitalized for ten years after that. Ten years' of going to the hospital. I feel bad saying this, but I sometimes thought, "What am I living for?"

After his condition had improved a little, I took him to the beach in Yumoto by car. Yumoto is known for its beautiful sunset. I wanted to show it to him. He gazed at the sun setting through the window of the passenger seat.

"The sunset is beautiful? Don't be silly," he said, "The rising sun is much more beautiful."

Before his illness, he used to go off to the sea on his squid boat at night, and come back to the port early in the morning. He must have seen the sun rising every day.

He kept gazing at the western sky until the sun set completely. In his mind's eye, he was probably looking at the sunrise.

Next year will be the thirteenth anniversary of my husband's death. I realize I am already over eighty. These days my physical condition often fails me. I have not been back to Akita since my brother passed away five years ago. I no longer wish to return there. Even so, I sometimes remember the old days.

Snow, books, and the balloons.

Mother and Child

I came to Morotsu from Katsumoto when I was twenty-one years old. I was born on the 1st January, 1929 in Higashi-hamlet in Katsumoto. I was the first born and had three brothers. My mother passed away when I was seventeen.

According to my mother, I was just being given my first bath when a postman came delivering New Year's cards. He said, "What a happy event to have a baby on New Year's Day!" When I was told this by my mother, I asked doubtfully, "Are you sure? Was I really born on that day? Maybe you made it up because it sounds better." But she replied, "It's true. You were really born on that day." I assume it must be true.

My father was a farmer, but he became sick and was too weak to work during his thirties and forties. When I was in the sixth grade, I made a straw-futon for him, because regular futons at that time were so heavy, not like those we have now. He suffered from spinal caries. He was so thin that the top of his spine stuck out.

As it was difficult to treat him on the island, he used to pay regular visits to a doctor in Fukuoka. A passenger ship used to call at Katsumoto then, and a small barge was used to carry passengers to and from the ship. I remember seeing my grandfather and my uncle taking turns to carry my father along the road on their backs.

I was only a child, so my memories are hazy. My mother had a weak heart. It wasn't so bad when she was young, but as she grew older it got worse.

She used to work for another farm as a day labourer, and earned a little money, a few yen or less, I'm not sure the exact amount as it was old money. We were so poor. One of my grandfathers lived with us. He was a heavy drinker, he just drank and drank. I heard he used to be a hard worker when he was younger. My mother had to pay for his drink. A nearby store used to sell small bottles of shochu. We were often given 25-sen and sent to buy it. My mother's life was a struggle until she finally passed away the year the war ended. Much later when our life became better and we became able to afford to buy things, I wished that my mother were still alive, I wished I could give her everything she didn't have in her life and put good food on her plate.

As our quality of life improved, my father's health recovered, and he started to work at the post office. He became a postman. He was still not strong enough for farm work, but was just about able to deliver letters. After some time when he became stronger, he started fishing. He bought a boat and fixed an outboard motor to it.

My father lived to be a hundred and two years and seven months old. "My body lost all its muscles because of spinal caries, but then started anew. That is why I have managed to live this long," he used to say. His mind remained clear, never showing any sign of senility.

He passed his final month or so in hospital. It was August. His great-grandson was going to get married in November. The moment he heard the news, he said, "I won't live that long. Please immediately send him my wedding gift." "What are you talking about, you still look very well," we all protested. "I may look well on the outside, but I can feel my body is giving up on me. Please hurry! Please send it today, the sooner the better," he insisted. He died three days later.

Until the last moment he had a clear head and was able

to do everything by himself including going to toilet. On his last day, I tried to put him in a diaper, but he rejected it. He used a urinal without making any mess. His hospital room had three other patients. On his final morning, he went to each of them and said, "Thank you for being kind." He passed away just after eight that evening.

When the war started, I was learning sewing at school. Because of the war, there was a recruitment drive to find volunteers to help construct fortress for some cannons. I started working there at the age of sixteen. Every day we traveled to a small island called Nagarasu just beyond the Wakamiya lighthouse in Katsumoto.

I used to leave home at five or six in the morning. Those who came from afar had to get up as early as three. Every morning we took a boat to the island. There were four cannon turrets. We had to carry sand, cement, gravel, and ballasts from the port. The distance from the seaside to the site was about one kilometer, and we carried the cargo using carts. There was an ox on the island. I took hold of the ox by its mouth and used it to pull my cart. When I meet people who I knew from that time, they still mention to me how good I was with the ox.

We sang songs together, "Maitah, maitah, sora maitah⋯," as some pulled and others pushed the carts, and finally we completed the four turrets. We dug secret tunnels to connect them, which was quite dangerous work and led to some injuries.

The commanding officer was 28 years old and not from the island. He was an outsider. He must have had some sort of higher education to be in command. Those working under him were usually older than him, and they resented the way they were treated.

Occasionally a B29 came flying overhead. The officer used to watch the planes using his binoculars. We in turn watched the officer from below where we were camouflaging the cannons. "Now what should we do, kill the officer or shoot down the plane?"

The war ended, without the guns ever been fired in anger. "What a waste after all that hard work!" Tears were shed.

The officer disappeared. He must have feared for his life. He hid himself and during the night sneaked out of Nagarasu.

After the end of the war, my mother died, and two years passed. My father introduced us to his second wife. She was from Morotsu. She told me about a family near her parents' house. An old blind man and his wife were living with their son, a widower, and his child. The child was born in February, and in October his mother passed away. My step mother asked me if I could go and help them with the housework. That is the reason I came here to Morotsu.

The boy was two years old when I arrived. His father Yukio had just recovered from the pleura, and was not working. During my three years working for them, the boy, Shoji or Sho as he was known, slowly became attached to me, and started to call me 'Mommy'. At this point his grandmother asked me to stay with them permanently. The child was motherless and I was worried if his father were to marry again, what kind of woman would she be? I felt pity for the boy, and decided I could put up with Yukio and remain for the child's sake.

They held a simple wedding ceremony for me. I was

twenty-four. I later had three children of my own. So including Sho, I had four boys to bring up.

At the beginning of our married life, my husband wasn't well enough to work much. As his health improved, he started to go squid fishing. He farmed and fished. We grew wheat, and soy beans. Our fields were scattered, here and there. The farthest away was in Taiso-hamlet. He even went to Tottori Prefecture to work in construction to earn more money. So we were able to afford to send our sons to university. My husband passed away at ninety-four. He was twelve years older than me. How many years have passed since he died? It must be seven, as I am now eighty-nine.

My husband never listened to me, even when I complained about his mother. He was indifferent to such things. He was reticent and didn't talk much, but we sometimes quarreled. After a particularly big fight, I decided to leave bundling together what I could. I started heading home to my parent's house, but the thought of Sho and how he might feel stopped me in my tracks. I decided to return, only to find my husband was already fast asleep.

Sho did not know that he was born of a different mother from his other brothers until he was in sixth grade of elementary school. That is when schools require various information about the students' family before they enter Junior high school. His grandmother kept saying, "I detest the boy, because he is the child of my son's former wife." It was so painful to hear.

I didn't want him to feel that he was treated unfairly. So I bought him anything he wanted. I used to go to collect sea urchins and sell them. I kept the money for myself and saved it. My other three boys always wore hand-me-downs. Whenever I attended memorial services or any ceremonial occasions, we used to receive cake to take home, we used to share it. I always made sure Sho's portion was bigger than other boys. They used to complain. "Never mind! He is bigger, so he gets more. You can have more when you grow bigger."

However his grandmother, my mother-in-law, kept repeating how much she didn't like the boy, whenever my husband wasn't around. She was really hard on the boy. I came to understand that her cruelty was probably the result of her also being badly treated by her own mother-in-law. My husband is the child of this first marriage. Her first husband died young because of illness. She was then forced to marry her brother-in-law. He was a mean man. When he was younger, he was bitten by a snake and blinded. She had never wanted to marry him but was given no choice by her mother-in-law. "Marry him or lose your child."

My mother-in-law was so mean. She tormented me. I found it so difficult to cope with her that I often felt I'd be better off dead. I felt I was the only one who suffered like this. However, I heard about a mother and her child in Ebisu, who jumped from a cliff down into the sea. They jumped during the sports day at Seto Elementary School. So everyone could see from the top of the hill the two floating corpses. As the crowd watched, the mother's corpse drifted towards the child. Such a shame! When I heard the story, I felt a deep sorrow for them and wished I could have died in their place.

Once when Sho was taking a bath, I think it was about the time he was in sixth grade, he asked me to heat up the water as it was not warm enough. So I lit a fire in the firebox outside the bathroom. While I was preparing the fire, I couldn't help myself, and started crying, and told Sho what my mother-in-law had said to me. Then he said, "People like her haven't been to school, so they say uneducated things. Don't worry, I know what she is like." I gained strength from his words, and decided never to complain about her again. Not once. Sometimes I cried alone, though.

I never answered back to my mother-in-law, but when Shoji became twenty-two, I could no longer put up with her. I said to her, "I came here when he was only two. Whatever I have done, however much I've tried, you have always hated him. I have had enough. I'm taking him with me." Looking slightly shocked, she said, "You've been here that long? Yes, so you have. I'm really very sorry. Please don't leave and please forgive me." And then she told Shoji to be good to his mother and not to fight with his brothers. "Even after I die, I will be looking over you," she added and from that day she changed her attitude towards him. She passed away at eighty-eight.

As my children were all boys, I used to tell them to find a kind-hearted girl to marry. I also said, "I don't mind who it is as long as you like her." I was so content when Shoji married a nice girl.

Now I live as I please. I go to play gate-ball on Mondays, Wednesdays, and Fridays. I go on a trip whenever I feel like it. I still work in the field and grow vegetables, on Tuesdays, Thursdays, and Saturdays. Actually, I've just returned from the field. Potatoes and onions.

I came to Morotsu at twenty-one, so now nearly 70 years

have passed. I wouldn't have come here if it weren't for Shoji. I haven't told this to him, so I don't know how he would feel about it.

The Prom

I was born in Kabankalan, Negros Occidental in the Philippines.

Negros Occidental is situated in the Visayan Islands between Luzon Island and Mindanao Island. It takes forty-five minutes by air from Manila, and from the airport another five hours by car. Sugar cane, corn plantations and rice paddies are everywhere. I was the first born amongst nine children, and had four younger brothers and four younger sisters.

My father was a farmer. He had a small piece of land and grew sugar cane and eggplants. He now has rice paddies too, as my third brother Robert bought three hectors of agricultural land. Robert lives in London working at St. George's Hospital as a head nurse.

I was brought up in a poor family. Trying to remember the old days is, to be honest, quite painful for me. We were a big family and really poor. When I was at college, I had to take a one-year leave of absence from school because I could not pay my fee. I somehow managed to graduate after five years. It was no easy matter for me to continue to study in that environment. I studied education at Kabankalan Catholic College, and became a teacher after graduation. However, in the fourth year of my career, in 1989, there was an attempted coup, and the school I was working for shut down. I came to Japan two years later.

I think I was an active girl when I was a child, always running about and often climbing trees. I picked wild flowers or fruits. There were bananas and guava everywhere. I also liked swimming in the nearby river. I collected beautiful stones in many different colours. My father used to carve woods to make us toys as he could not afford to buy them for us. We used to play with anything we could get our hands on. Even bottle caps could serve as a fine toy.

We did not have a TV. To start with we did not have any electricity. When we needed light, we used candles. It does not mean that there was no electricity in the whole town, but we just could not afford it.

My house had a tin roof, so when we had heavy rain, it made such a noise. If it rained hard during the night, I could not sleep at all. The kitchen roof was made of coconut leaves. So on rainy nights I used to sit in the kitchen and gaze into the darkness beyond.

I never took a packed lunch to school. I always returned home as all my schools from elementary school to college were very close to my house. I liked a dish called Adobo, a typical Philippine home cooked food made with chicken and pork, spices, garlic, vinegar, pepper, and vegetables, with a little sugar and coconut milk. It was eaten in summer and good for giving you stamina against the heat.

After I entered high school, I became introverted. More precisely I cut myself off from my schoolmates. They enjoyed chatting in restaurants or cafes after school with the pocket money given to them by their parents. But I did not have any money. I would go straight back home as soon as school was over to help my parents. I was the first born child and had eight brothers and sisters. I was not in a position to enjoy my time as young people usually did. So now I keep telling my children to enjoy themselves as much as they can whenever they have the chance. I was very responsible. I never thought about boys. Most adolescent girls dream of dating a handsome boy, don't they? But not me, I was bound by a heavy sense of responsibility.

There were some classmates who said, "Judy, let's go swimming," or "Why don't we go out to the town." But I always turned them down. I had no time to waste on such things. When I reached the final year of high school, I suddenly realized that my teens had been terrible, and this could not be right. So I decided to go to college. I told myself I should not take my responsibilities too seriously. I should start enjoying life more. Until then I had never thought that way. I only thought I had to be a good big sister. Then I studied hard and successfully entered college. I realized that studying was what I wanted to do most.

I liked children, so I chose the department of education.

The impression of my college life? It may have been a little different from what I had imagined. I cannot simply state it was fun, or it was boring. At that time I felt a barrier between myself and other people. First of all I had to worry about paying my school fee. I could not pay on time, and had to beg the office to extend the deadline. My father tried hard to squeeze it out of his earnings, and managed, even though it was delayed, to pay somehow. Scholarships did not exist in those days. Finally I managed to graduate.

Learning itself gave me pure pleasure. The professors were all foreigners, English, American and other nationalities. I liked talking with them. I frequented the library and spent my time studying and reading novels, as I did not have any money to buy books. Other students hung around in groups or went out on dates. But I did not. I put all my energy into my studies.

The college had social clubs similar to Fraternities or Sororities in the States. Once a senior student invited me to such a club, and I tried, but soon I realized it was not my cup of tea. They always seemed to be so enthusiastic about life, going out drinking, making campfires on the beach, and having boyfriends. They always seemed to be putting on a show. Even when they quarreled, it was, how can I put it, fake, fake quarrels. Anyway I hated it all.

To be frank, somewhere in the back of my mind, I wanted to have a boyfriend. I wondered what it would be like to be in love. But I did not have any chance. I wanted to have a boyfriend, but at the same time I feared that if I fell in love, it might destroy me. I entered college hoping to enjoy myself, but I found myself fearing such pleasure.

However, in the third year I fell in love with a professor. Mr. Milford. I liked his way of teaching. He was an English man, 47, and single. He did not seem to have a girlfriend. I was twenty-one years old then. There was a mango tree besides the chapel in college. I used to read books under the tree. He sometimes came there and stopped in front of me.

"Judy, why are you always alone? What do you pray for in the chapel? Why are you always in the library? Everyone hangs around in group. Why are you sitting there reading?"

He asked me many questions.

I just said, "Please stop asking me questions. Sir, you don't know anything about my life," despite the fact of how much I liked him.

I shall never forget the prom on Valentine's Day in February of that year. I danced with a man for the first time in my life. It was held in the gym which was decorated with balloons and paper tapes, and the band was made up of members of the music club. All the students and teachers were there.

I was unusually dressed up in a long red dress, and so I felt a little nervous. I was talking with my classmates when Mr. Milford appeared in a linen suit. He held out his right hand to me. I still remember the music that was being played at that time. The King and Queen of Hearts. While dancing my hands were trembling.

After the dance, he guided me to a chair, and asked me, "Would you like something to drink?" I said, trying to stand, "I'll go and get it." Shaking his head he said, "No, I will." We toasted with fruit cocktails. He took my hand before leaving, of course just a handshake between a teacher and a student, and said, "In the future when you meet a man, you should try not to be so nervous. And if you come to like him, don't be shy and tell him so. If you don't, you will feel sorry. You will be fine."

He probably said this because he must have imagined that I was nervous and shy in front of all men. That was partly true, but real reason I was trembling was because I was dancing with him. But I could not tell him what I really felt. Love affairs between teachers and students were forbidden.

Mr. Milford continued to be kind to me. Once when I was reading under the tree, he bought me ice cream. He sent me a Christmas card, which said "You are a very good student." But I couldn't send him a card in return because I didn't have money to buy one.

The final time I saw him was an evening just before my

graduation. I went back to the library to get something I had left. Mr. Milford happened to be there among some other teachers. He was to leave for England that year.

I approached him, and said, "Good evening, sir." "What are you doing?" he asked me looking surprised. I said, "I'm here just to pick up something I forgot." "Shall we go for a little walk?" he said.

We walked in the evening campus. I said, "Thank you for the kindness you have shown me," and extended my hand. Then touching my hair he said, "Good luck." Tears rolled down my cheek. I started to run and stopped under the mango tree beside the chapel. He came running after me. I said, "I like you." "I like you more," he replied.

I can still hear his words. It was the last time I would see him. Soon after that he left for England without attending the graduation ceremony.

After the graduation, I started to teach at the elementary school I had attended. However in the second year, I caused some trouble. In my fifth grade class, there was a restless boy who always gave me a hard time. His father was a policeman, and he was an only child. A policeman in the countryside was quite a nuisance. The boy always carried a big spider with him. He kept the spider in a match box, and would let it out to play. I could not concentrate on my teaching. So I told him, "Don't bring a spider into class. It's impossible to study, isn't it?" Then he replied obediently, "All right, Miss."

The following day in the classroom, he came up to my desk and said, "I need to pee." I said, "OK," and continued the class. Two hours later he still had not returned. I went looking for him, and found him playing with the spider behind the school building. I told him off again. He, again, replied obediently, "Yes, Miss," without paying any attention. The following afternoon, half the class did not appear. I rushed behind the building, and found, as I had suspected, the boy playing with his spider surrounded by his classmates. I saw the spider crawling on the ground, and in a rage I whacked it with my hand.

I should not have done that. I still regret it. The children must have been shocked. A teacher should be teaching children how to be kind to living things, but instead I had killed a spider in front of them. I was young. I could not control my feelings. The boy started to cry and ran off home.

The next day the boy's father came into the classroom. He was wearing his uniform. It was in the middle of a lesson, but he glared at me saying, "I want to have a word with you. Let's go outside." I was taken to the principal's office, where he started to shout at me in front of the principal. Then I was told to step outside and wait. Before long the father left the office and I was called in again.

The principal said, "I would like to transfer you to another school." "To a school in the mountain," he added.

I was demoted.

People there were simple and bighearted. Fathers and Mothers were kind, and there were no policemen. Nobody came to PTA meetings, so if there was something to convey, I had to visit them and tell them directly. Writing did not work as most adults in the region could not read.

After about two years working at the school, there was a national coup. Eventually it ended in failure, but schools shut down and lessons could not continue. Wages were not paid for many months, and finally we were locked out of the school. I gave up my teaching job, and decided to go to Manila, the capital city, because there were no jobs available in the country. I badly needed money to support my parents, my brothers and my sisters.

In Manila, a lot of people came from all over the country seeking jobs. Finding jobs was indeed like a battle of survival. Although I had my college qualification, it was from an unknown local college. Anyone who was in charge of employment chose graduates from famous universities like Athens University and Philippine University. I knew that from the beginning. But I had to find something. So I applied for a cleaning job. In the application form there was a list of different jobs to choose from. I could have chosen a better job with higher wages. But I intentionally chose one at the bottom of the list. In that way I managed to get an interview at an import company with its main office in California. The interviewer asked me, "Why are you applying to be a cleaner, when you have a good education."

"I really need a job. I have to support my family," I replied.

I was immediately hired and given a uniform there and then, together with a complete set of cleaning equipment including a vacuum-cleaner. As a matter of fact I did not even know how to use it. We did not have any electric appliances at home.

Mr. Barns, the president of the company, was 63 years old but looked much younger. He was a well-dressed smart gentleman. His work took him back and forth between

Manila and California. He often drank coffee in the office. It was his secretary's duty to prepare it. When he changed his secretary, the new one did not learn quickly how to make coffee or the best timing to serve it. So I told her. Somehow I had picked it up as I was cleaning his office. He must have noticed. One day when I was dusting his desk, he lifted his cup and said, "Thank you." He asked me, "What's your name?" "Judy," I replied. "Well, my daughter's name is Judy, too," he said smiling. From that day on we often spoke.

One occasion Mr. Barns invited me to a casino. There were mountains of food, fruits and brownies. It was like a dream to me. I devoted myself to eating. Mr. Barns called me from afar, "Judy, come here." "No, sir," I continued to stick to the food corner.

Then I was introduced to a friend of him, an American man of 80 years of age. I was told that he also had an import company like Mr. Barns. He was thinking of retiring soon and live in comfort. He was a widower and wanted to marry a young Filipina. "I want to marry you," he said to me whom he had just met. He also said that I could go to America with him and live leisurely in a large house. If I had been an ambitious woman, I might have leapt at the offer. But I declined politely.

When I went to the casino with Mr. Barns for the second time, that same American man proposed to me again. Again I declined politely. I was afraid that Mr. Barns might have been offended it, but instead I seemed to have gained his confidence.

"Judy, I would like you to work in a more responsible position from tomorrow," he said. And I was appointed to be a team leader of market research. My salary rose considerably. I worked hard. The work itself was interesting. I would go to a supermarket and check the expiry date of a certain product, say chocolate from a certain company. We would find out how soon the product was consumed, and make a report with our interpretation and suggestions of the data. I worked in that position for almost a year.

I rented an apartment near my office. My landlady's husband who was Japanese, introduced me to a man, who is now my husband. My husband had a construction company on Iki-island. At that time he visited the Philippines to find Filipino workers for his company. The landlady's husband was helping him.

He was 43 years old then. I was 27. He was the same age as my mother, so I was a little reluctant at first. But when I actually met him, I found him to be nice. He was kind and gentleman-like. I was not interested in the 80-year-old American, but he seemed like a better option. And by marrying him, I could do my duty to my family.

His original plan to find Filipino workers did not go well, but instead he found his better half and returned to the island with her. It was my first visit to another country. It was not easy to get used to the life on the island, but on the whole I enjoyed myself. I was able to send money to my family in the Philippines every month, and along the way I gave birth to two daughters.

The older daughter is now a graduate student, and lives in Fukuoka. As she did well at college, she did not have to pay all her school fees. The younger one now goes to a vocational college, also in Fukuoka, wanting to become a flight attendant.

My husband and I have different opinions on the children's education. He says, "Women don't need to study." He thinks women should marry and support her husband. But I don't agree. I am a woman and I went to college. Even though I was poor, I believed education was more important than anything else. The differences in our opinions still exist. I am sure the direction I gave to my daughters was right. It cannot be wrong.

When my first daughter was five years old, I was asked to help at an elementary school with the English lessons. I willingly accepted the offer. The text book was not sufficient, so I tried to make it more fun, by teaching the children Philippine plays or cooking. At first it was not paid, but then I was offered the job officially by the local government. I was involved in English teaching for 18 years.

I quit the job at the elementary school two years ago, and started a nursing job. After that I worked in the kitchen at a nursing home. My brother Robert who is a head nurse in England will soon return to the Philippines and open a nursing college there. I would like to help him if the opportunity arises. My experiences in Japan will certainly be very useful. This is why I started to do nursing work. I do not mind even after I get older, even as a volunteer, I would love to help. I want to pass on my experiences to young Filipinos. I believe it will certainly be useful for the future of the Philippines.

Once every two years I return to my home in Negros Occidental. My daughters do not want to come with me any longer. They do not seem to like the country so much. I cannot blame them considering its poor environment and inconveniences. They were not born there and never lived there. But I want to die there. I told them so, and they said, "That is OK, Mom." As a matter of fact, I have already prepared my grave at home.

My father died of acute cardiac infarction eight years ago. A little too early, isn't it? He was a heavy smoker and loved drinking. He continued working at his farm until his final day. Now our youngest brother Fabian is looking after the farm.

In the past we did not have sufficient enough rice. My mother used to add a lot of water to make it into a kind of porridge. So Robert and I made a promise that we would do our best to support our family in the future, so that they would not suffer, and would be able to eat rice, not porridge. Since I came to the island, I have been able to send money back home every month. Now all my family eat properly cooked rice, not porridge.

I am not entirely satisfied with my present life. There are things that do not go well. But I think I was able to achieve something. I take pride in that.

Fusuma - Paper Doors

The Chinshin-Ryu is a Japanese tea ceremony school. The school and its methods were originated and performed by the samurai class. It taught the art of strength and elegance. After half a century, I still have a lot to learn. I often wonder why I have devoted so much of my time to it. I used to instinctively dislike discipline, but perhaps somewhere in my mind I must have been searching for some.

My grandmother on my mother's side taught me basic manners, starting from the right way to open and close fusuma-doors.

"You must behave well when you go to Sasebo. When you are visiting someone, never allow your manners to let you down."

She was very strict on a girl of only seven. "Why do I have to learn this?" My grandmother's answer was clear. "Because Taeko, you are a naval officer's daughter."

I had to rigorously practice, how to stand up, how to sit down, and how to praise the flower arrangement on the tokonoma, an alcove, in the tea room. Eventually I was able to put on a kimono by myself.

My mother was good at kimono making. She took my measurements and made many kimonos for me. My neighbors would talk to me whenever they saw me on my way to and from school, "Taeko, you are so lucky to have so many different kimonos to wear."

I used to walk back from school joining hands with four or five friends from the neighborhood. We walked together as far as a local shrine and from there we waved good bye and set off on our way. "See you tomorrow." I cannot forget the view of the island seen from the grounds of the shrine. The line of the mountain ridge, the ears of rice waving in the wind, the sky and the sea meeting in the distance.

When I was in the second year of elementary school, my father returned from his ocean journeys. We left the island and a new life in Sasebo began. My father belonged to the defense corps. Our rented house was behind the station. There were no rice fields to be seen. Many of the town's streets were paved with stones. I could hear the sound of my father's footsteps echoed in our house as he approached.

"Listen! Your father is coming home."

As a family, we sat on the floor waiting for him to enter. I sat next to my mother with my younger sister and still infant brother, we all bowed respectfully with three fingers of each hand in front of us on the floor, "Welcome back."

My father would hand his short sword to my mother, and then take off and arrange his military boots. My sister would whisper, "Look at the way they treat his short sword! His rank is low but somehow he makes himself appear to be so important, doesn't he?" She had no self-restrain, she did and said exactly as she pleased. As she closed the fusuma door of her room, my father's voice was heard shouting, "Do it again!" He was very aware of the sound of a door being carelessly closed. I tried to be careful, so it was always my sister who got scolded. She would try again and say, "Is this OK?" "Not good enough. Do it again." My father would not put up with half measures. So my sister was made to repeat the same thing over and over again, until in the end somehow I got scolded, too.

My mother usually did not argue with my father, but she

spoke up for me when she felt he was being unfair.

"It's not Taeko's fault. You always scold her for no reason."

"It's because she is the first born. As long as we educate the first child well, the other children will follow her example."

So, to be honest, I didn't like my father.

When he was in a good mood, he would make me sit beside him as he smoked his cigarettes saying, "Taeko, you don't like me, do you?" Even a child can tell a lie. "Yes, I do."

"Oh, really?" he would nod.

"Do you want to study anything?" he asked me.

"I want to learn the piano."

"You ask for the impossible. We are not wealthy enough for that. If I am promoted to a higher rank, I will be able to pay for your lessons, but now I can't."

"I want to learn calligraphy."

My father was a skillful writer.

"Good, you want to learn calligraphy? I fully approve of that."

I continued to go to calligraphy classes for the remainder of my time at elementary school.

After moving to Sasebo, my mother made me a new kimono.

"As you are a new student, put on this kimono for School."

Children on the island used to wear kimonos, but in Sasebo they wore western clothes.

"No, I don't want to wear a kimono any more."

"Kimonos are good. You should wear it properly and tie your Obi. You should go to school dressed smartly."

Even as a child, I could sense that my homeroom teacher was anxious about whether her new student from the island could adjust to Sasebo. She was young, and could easily be mistaken for a student.

"Try to solve this problem," she said handing me a piece of chalk. While I was writing the answer on the blackboard, she asked me something which had nothing to do with arithmetic, "How did you get your kimono? Did your mother make it for you?"

"Yes, she did."

"I see." She said, and continued the lesson.

I felt hurt at first as I thought she was laughing at my kimono, but I was wrong.

I was appointed the class sub-leader. It was a customary that the leader was a boy, and the sub-leader a girl. The leader wore a badge wrapped with dark-red woolen yarn, the sub-leader's badge was wrapped with both dark-red and white yarn. While wearing the badge, I no longer felt ashamed of wearing my kimono.

My favourite subject was music. I loved singing. During the break, I used to sing the songs which we had practiced, with friends. My favourite songs were Red Bird Little Bird, and Oboro Zukiyo (A night with a hazy moon). Every time I sang these songs, I remembered the island; the view from the grounds of the shrine, of mirror-like water-filled rice fields reflecting the clouds.

"Taeko, are you on your way home? Come here, come, come just for a moment!" one of the neighbors called me over. I followed her.

"I have many dumplings. Take some and eat them with your mother." She handed me some of them wrapped in a taro leaf. I thanked her and rushed home. Running at full speed on a footpath between rice fields, thinking of my mother's smiling face.

Even now by just singing those songs, the sight of those days spreads out vividly in my mind. In fact, that place hasn't changed much even now. Every time I pass there, I cannot but admire the beautiful view. As I look at it, those old school songs come to me again. And then somehow I become sentimental.

My father never realized his wish of promotion. By the time I had finished elementary school, he had left the Navy and got a job at the post office. Four year later, he had a stroke and passed away so suddenly without any forewarning. It was just before the Greater East Asian War broke out. After he left the Navy, his mood softened. I felt sorry for him.

I acquired a teaching qualification at the teacher's training school in Omura, and started to work at an elementary school on Iki-island. When I was twenty-three, I married a teacher who worked at the same school as me, he was 12 years older than I. He was a widower, and had three children. Everyone around me was opposed to us, but I was determined to marry him. I thought there was no other man but him. Maybe I had a little bit of a rebellious streak. My father was so strict, but my husband was kind and understanding.

I started taking tea ceremony lessons on my mother-in-law's advice when I was well over thirty. "Chinshin-ryu might be good for you, as it has been practiced by the samurai class." The real reason she encouraged me was because she was learning the tea ceremony herself. But that didn't matter because I soon became completely absorbed in it. I became dedicated to it whilst also working and bringing up children at the same time, until I finally qualified as a master of the tea ceremony.

Since then I have continued the tea ceremony for sixty years as a teacher. During the time so many things have come to happen. Yet now at ninety-four, what I can remember is the fact that I have continued teaching the Chinshin-ryu almost every Saturday without exception. Only once when my husband died of lung cancer was I so disheartened that I couldn't do anything and even started to think of giving up the tea ceremony. When I couldn't find any meaning in life, I received a call from a doctor in a port town on the island, whom I had become acquainted with through a cultural club.

"Taeko, can you come over now?"

"What can I do for you?"

"Never mind. Just come."

The doctor had a hanging scroll opened in his study. On the scroll a white calligraphy paper was already mounted, but nothing was written yet. The doctor was known also as a calligrapher.

"I am going to write on this. If you like it, you can have it. Take it home with you."

"Doctor, it is more than I deserve."

"Don't worry. But I can only do it once, so I may make a mistake."

The doctor smiled and held a brush.

山花迎客咲
谷鳥避人啼

The flowers in the mountain bloom to welcome visitors,
Birds in the valley sing for themselves.

I returned home and hung the scroll that I had been just
given on the tokonoma of the tea room. After a long while,
I heated an iron teakettle. Two spoonfuls of powdered green
tea from the caddy. Pour hot water and whip.

I sipped tea with my back straight. Strongly and elegantly.

Roppei

'Roppei' is the name of my restaurant. The counter was here, and the kitchen was over there. Everyone called me Roppei. Even though it's not my real name, I decided to use it as the name of my restaurant.

I have been interested in photography since I was young, but I didn't have enough money to buy a camera. Cameras were far too expensive for me. Mr. Masumoto Kingo was the first person to own a camera around here. Nobody else had a camera before him. He had a good camera with bellows. He took a picture of us when we were about five. Look, this one here. Nobody could take a picture as good as this then, around 1940. This one here is the first photograph that I took. No, it's not a passenger ship, but a type of an American ship known as a flash-boat.

During my childhood, a ship called Isao-maru carried both cargo and passengers between mainland and Iki-island. It couldn't carry cars like the ships of today, and the engine wasn't diesel but semi-diesel. Fishing boats also had the same type of engine. There were Semi-diesel engines and diesel ones. With semi-diesel engines you first have to warm them up and then let them go. The small furnace must be constantly kept heated. Diesel engines explode with compression power and are far more powerful.

In those days ships could not come alongside the pier, so they anchored offshore and barges were used for the final stretch. The barges were made of wood and we called them 'Haseke'. The journey to Fukuoka by Isao-maru took about six hours. Taishu-maru which replaced Isao-maru had a diesel engine and took about four and a half hours. Now it only takes an hour.

In the past we used barges even when we were going to Ashibe which is the neighboring town, as there wasn't a bridge then. The boatmen were mostly old. Born in a fishing village we learned to row boats from a very young age, so we couldn't just sit there as passengers, we helped row the boat for the boatmen. The barges were managed by Mr. Satomi Katsuyoshi who later became the chairman of the fishermen's association, and also the village mayor.

The war continued until the middle of my fourth year of elementary school. So up until the third year we received a war-time style education. Both semaphore and Morse code were compulsory subjects. Towards the end of the war, soldiers were stationed around here and sometimes semaphore was used by them. We would watch and laugh, pointing out their mistakes. We were better than them. I even had a regulation style flag.

I only became really aware of the war when it was just about to end. The enemy fighter planes appeared from over that mountain. We were at school and an air-raid alarm was sounded. Every one ran into the woods, because we knew that staying in the schoolhouse was dangerous. I was a bad student, and I really wanted to see the fighter planes. So I ran into the sweet potato field and lay on my back between furrows and covered myself with the sweet potato vines. At that moment there was a huge roar overhead. I saw two of them, Grumman fighters.

Although some people had to flee from the machine-gun fire, no one was killed. Probably their target was the anchored naval ships and the helicopter corps in Tsutsuki. We used to call the corps "the autogiro." We had to donate eggs to nourish them. We took the eggs, which were to be given to them, to school, but we weren't happy about it. So we used to mockingly say, "Autogiro nan-giro, tamago kuroute nan-giro (Autogiro, eating eggs, what's that all about?)" Of course we didn't say it openly. If they had heard, we would have been in deep trouble.

I am on close terms with your family. Your grandfather, Yasutaro used to have another small clinic just across from here, at which he worked twice a week. My grandfather used to call on him frequently, probably just to have a chat.

Hiroki is Yasutaro's heir. Hiroki's house and his clinic stand on the hill over there. They were built when I was in elementary school. My grandfather was involved in the construction, as it was during the war. He was a fisherman, but he was also a member of the school committee. There was some open space between the Seto Elementary School houses, where they decided to build an auditorium. Machines needed to prepare the lumber for the building materials used a lot of oil which was hard to procure at that time. As it was a school building they somehow managed to acquire the oil. And my grandfather arranged to have the wood needed to build the clinic sawn together with the school wood.

On my grandfather's final day, both Dr. Yasutaro and Dr. Hiroki visited him. They saw that there was no hope of him recovering. Then my grandfather said, "My life is nearly over, but please help me to breathe freely just once." He was suffocating. "I won't say that you killed me." That's what I was told by my father. They must have given him some kind of injection. He was actually able to breathe, and after the doctors left he passed away peacefully.

The branch clinic was later converted into a bar by Mr. Kakimoto, but it burned down. This area was a busy section of the town, my restaurant Roppei was here, Coffee shop Riru was on the other side, and a snack bar Taiyo was next door. All of them are gone now.

There was a cinema "Shurakukan", just 50 meters away from here. We often went there. It was often used for plays and traditional Naniwa-bushi performances too. I sometimes went to see movies with my wife. It was there until I was twenty-seven or twenty-eight. I have special memories of Shurakukan. These days the cultural festival of Junior high school is often held at a training hall in the Rito center. But we used to do a double performance at the schoolhouse, once for the fishermen and once for the farmers. However, it was always a busy time for the fishermen and as a result nobody turned up. I thought it was such a shame after all the practicing and preparation. So after persuading the schoolmaster and the chairman of the Parents' Association, we decided to use the cinema. I negotiated with the cinema, and said that I would take responsibility. They agreed to let us use it for free. It's quite unheard of to have a Junior high school festival at night, isn't it? I did everything from the opening speech to the cleaning up afterwards. It was so much fun like a big festival.

This picture was taken at a sumo meet. I was slim but a good sumo wrestler. I took part in the junior high school district meet. I lost in an individual match, and I was very upset. But then someone organized another competition, based on winning three straight fights or five straight fights, both with prize money, three hundred yen and five hundred yen respectively. I wanted the money, so I entered and won both. The prize money enabled me to go on a school trip which I otherwise couldn't afford.

When I was in junior high school, the bus from Katsumoto only ran as far as Tanie. From Tanie we had to walk. My father and I often went to Fukuoka and my father's boss would entrust us with one million yen which we would bring back in a 18 litre-tin can. I sat on the can when I was on the ship and on the bus for fear of it being stolen. When someone asked me what it was, I answered, "It's something important." I was sitting on a million yen. A million yen at that time was really a large amount of money. The can would fit in the rucksack. From Tanie my father carried it on his shoulder, and whenever he put it down, I sat on it. The money was going to be used to buy dried cuttlefish, which were then sent to China, or should I say smuggled to China. I only helped to carry the money but was never involved in the smuggling. My father's boss was such a smart man.

The boss was known as Lieutenant Obayashi. This wasn't a soldier's ranking, but the ranking of the secret military agency that was based overseas, in China to be exact. He had a special connection with the Chinese people. Most of his men were from the secret agency.

He was very strict. His house was in Daimyo in Fukuoka, where the Kiyokawa Construction Company is based now. I was first taken to his house when I was in the first year of junior high school. It was a grand house, and I was surprised to see that the toilet had a tatami-floor. There was even a western style dining table. When he saw me eating, he said, "You were taught manners by your grandfather, weren't you?"

He was right, whenever my grandfather saw me eating with my elbows raised, he would hit me with a flyswatter made of hemp palm. He said that I was disturbing other people. He would also say, "Don't look around when you are eating, concentrate on your own rice bowl." Because of this I was well received by the boss.

Lieutenant Obayashi had many different kinds of businesses. As well as dried cuttlefish smuggling, he also fished mackerel. He used dynamite in the sea to catch the fish. The dynamite blew up with the sound 'Dong!', we scooped up mackerel (saba) with nets. They became known as 'Dong-saba.' In order to get permission to use dynamite from the American GHQ, he brought all the officials from their Kyushu Office in Fukuoka to the island to entertain them. They stayed here dispersed among the houses of the wealthy. There were fourteen or fifteen of them. They often played poker upstairs in Mr. Kuwamitsu's house. I used to help with handing out and shuffling the cards. I may have been the child who had most dealings with foreigners on the island. They stayed here for a week or so each time.

The GHQ office was in Akasakamon, Fukuoka. I often visited them on my way back from the boss. I used to be given cigarettes and chewing gum or snacks. I thought that they tasted so good as I had never had anything like that before.

My father used to go as far as Kagoshima to catch bonito on the boss's boat. One day, his boat overturned and sank. Luckily he was rescued by a passing ship. After that he returned to the island, where Mr. Kuwamitsu, a commercial fisherman who owned a lot of boats and nets, invited my father to work for him. He said to my father, "Isn't it about time you became a real fisherman?" My father worked for Mr. Kuwamitsu for the rest of his life. After I finished junior high school, I joined my father at Mr. Kuwamitsu's. This picture was taken around that time. The man standing here is my father.

Mr. Kuwamitsu was the boss of a fixed-net fishing fleet. His boats would leave around eight in the morning, once a day in September and October, and twice a day in marlin season, as the nets were easily broken. I worked as a fisherman for 15 years from the age of fifteen. I married at 23, and started my restaurant at 25. Soon the restaurant became my main concern.

I was a naughty young boy, but never a criminal. I have visited the police station several times, though. It was all part of growing up. I remember my father-in-law saying, "I can't hand over my daughter to such a bad guy." She was from Morotsu, and the road to Morotsu was so narrow. There was a better road if you went around the Ontakesan-mountain. On my wedding day I went to Morotsu to pick her up. I hired a small three-wheeled truck as there weren't any cars yet. It was raining, so I sat her in the seat next to the driver, and sat myself on the load-carrying platform, dressed in formal Japanese wear, holding an umbrella. By the time we reached home, I was soaking wet. In an attempt to be on time for the wedding, I had left home early in the morning, however our return journey took much longer than I had expected; heavy rain made the road muddy and the tyres needed to be chained. The guests had already arrived and were waiting for us. We had our wedding ceremony at home.

I opened my restaurant "Roppei" with my wife, it became quite popular. We served a variety of dishes from sushi to champon-noodles. There were about 600 households in Setoura. I was acquainted with almost all of them. I don't remember exactly when people started calling me Roppei. For some reason I don't have any pictures of my restaurant, maybe I was too busy at that time.

Around 1969 the Crown Prince visited Iki-Island. The roads were improved for his visit. They weren't like today's roads and the layer of asphalt was only surface deep. It was the first time a road had been paved on the island. The Prince later became the Heisei Emperor. He took lunch at the agricultural headquarters. Four of us including my cooking teacher prepared the lunch. To this day it is something that I am so proud of.

In 1960s, the fishing industry was doing very well. We got a big catch of mackerel pike. This is a picture of it. Isn't it amazing? We caught too much so the prices went down, eventually we caught more than we could sell. There were sardines, small ones. They were first boiled and then laid out to dry in the sun. Rows and rows of wire nets and bamboo shelves laden with dried sardines lined the coastline roads.

Yellowtail and squids. We started to fish yellowtail around six in the morning. But squid fishing took place at night, starting around five in the evening, and returning depending on the catch. The latest we would stay out was until early morning. When the catch was bad, we came back earlier.

Over the last twenty years, fish catches in Setoura have become increasingly poor. Most fishermen had no one to succeed them, so the streets of Setoura have become desolate.

Even the well-known fishermen, the men who held the fishery rights, the big bosses, Mr. Nasukawa, Mr. Kuwamitsu, and Mr. Sumino, had no successors.

I was advised to become a member of the town assembly, and many people supported me. At the election people could choose between writing my real name Shirakawa Norihiko or Roppei, my restaurant's name. The election administration accepted that both were valid. During my time at the assembly, I proposed and pressed on with the construction of that seawall over there. I thought the project was absolutely necessary.

Shortly after I became an assembly member, I became the juvenile probation officer. A senior officer said to me, "You are the one who needs to be on probation." I'll never be able to forget his words. My responsibility was to take care of those who were released on parole until they were due to report to the parole inspector to be judged. It was me who determined when they were ready to be judged. If I felt they deserved it, I recommended that their parole time might be reduced. I believe that everyone deserves a second chance.

You see, I did various things. I also worked as a member of the volunteer fire brigade. Once, when was it, maybe about 30 years ago, a group of elementary school children from Daimyo in Fukuoka visited Kuyoshi-beach. It was a windy day, the sea was dangerous. They were told not to swim in the water, just to play on the shore, but one boy went swimming regardless and was washed out to sea by the currents. His father who was present tried to rescue him. Three people were washed out to sea, the boy, his father and his teacher.

The beach had a history of drownings during rescue attempts. Once was when my father was young, during the Meiji period, and another was when I was in my teens. That time also involved a teacher trying to rescue a pupil. He managed to save the child, but despite his strong physique, his own strength gave out. There is a large monument on the beach in remembrance of him.

I happened to be at the town office on some business when I heard that some people were being carried away by the waves. Being a leader of the volunteer fire brigade, I rushed to the site. They were already far from shore. Whitecaps had formed and sea was very rough. I didn't know what to do, but soon realized that I had to do something. "Are there any life jackets?" I asked. "Yes, here!" A young man from the town office arrived. I asked him, "Are you a capable swimmer?" He answered, "Yes, I am." "Then, will you come with me?" "OK." he replied.

So we started to swim. He had just begun to work at the town office after finishing high school. I carried life jackets on my shoulder, but he started clinging to me and wouldn't let go. Then he tried to swim towards the tetrapod breakwater. I had to shout to stop him, and tell him that was the most dangerous direction to go. He must have been very nervous. So I handed him the life jackets, and together we swam out towards the victims. I gave the child a buoy and all together we swam farther away from the shore. I knew a rescue boat was coming, because I had called for it myself, without the rescue boat there would be no way of returning safely. When there is an undercurrent like there was in the past two cases, swimming away from the land was the only way to survive. The rescue boat finally arrived. First the young man from the town office, then the other three, and finally I, clambered aboard. I was covered with blood, because I had been badly knocked by the rocking boat. The father was almost unconscious, so I slapped him to keep him alert, otherwise he would have died. The boy was fine.

It was really a matter of life and death. A crowd of people had formed on the beach. When we returned to shore, there was only one member of the fire brigade waiting for us. I ordered him to go and get some blankets from nearby houses. I was quite annoyed, because we had some specially trained frogmen but they were nowhere to be seen. Unfortunately I learned that another boy was swept out to sea that day. The frogmen and other members of rescue service had tried to save him, but were unsuccessful in their search.

I received an award from the police. I had worked as a fisherman from a young age, and often been involved in accidents at sea. I was always prepared to tie a rope around myself and leap in to rescue someone.

It is rather embarrassing to say, but I once had to be rescued myself. It was the year before last. I was driving my car with my grandson, a junior high school student, sitting next to me. In front of my house, as you can see, is the sea. I was reversing and somehow my car fell straight into the sea. Just then, Mr. Tanabe happened to be passing by. He dived in there and then, and first saved my grandson and then me. I am so grateful to him. Mr. Tanabe works at the ironworks and is a member of the volunteer fire brigade. He is about 40 years old and a tall man, maybe about 190 cm. He is a surfer, and usually surfs at Kuyoshi Beach, the same beach that I saved the child.

I feel some kind of sense of fate.

The Horizon

Mr. Sakaguchi was born in 1921, and is now 96 years old. He lives in the Yahata Peninsula on the east of Iki-island. He joined the army at the age of nineteen in 1939. He was sent to the front in China, and returned home from Qingdao when the war ended. Recollecting the hardships of those days, he keeps repeating, "Even so I am still happier than those who were killed on the front."

The second son of a poor farmer, Mr. Sakaguchi was adopted by his aunt, at the same time as he entered elementary school. After he finished school, he started to work for the post office, but the salary was so low that he decided to sign up for the army. He was sent to a unit in Pyongyang, where he was given military training. The training was so severe, based on the assumption of an inevitable battle with Russian forces, that on the very first day he realized that he had made a mistake. However, luckily there was no active combat with Russia during his stay in Pyongyang.

He returned to Japan to a regiment in Fukuoka. From there, he was assigned to a ship heading for an unknown destination. The upper level officials revealed no information. Even company commanders were not told where they were heading for. The ship reached Pusan port. From there they took a train to Peking and marched westward.

In August of 1945, while he was in Shantung Province, he heard the news that the war had ended. However, his unit continued fighting until the following May. They were told that if they surrendered to the Chinese Nationalist forces, they would be treated amicably. But if they surrendered to the Communist forces they would end up in misery. Not knowing what to do, they continued to resist the Communists and headed south where they surrendered to the Nationalist. From there, they were moved on foot to Qingdao, where they were to be sent back to Japan by ship. On the way all their belongings were taken by the Chinese. They were left with nothing to eat or even water to drink. Some died of hunger. As it was impossible to take the corpses with them, they collected tree branches and twigs to burn the bodies, and then picked out finger bones which they kept in their mess kits. Even the mess kits were taken away as they were mistakenly thought to contain food.

Along the way they were joined by Japanese civilians who had worked on the railways or in mines. A woman who gave birth on the roadside had to abandon her baby. Nobody blamed her. Everyone just wanted to get home alive. They kept walking until they finally arrived at Qingdao. It was a long, harsh, miserable journey.

"Even so, I thought to myself, I was much luckier than those who died on the battle field."

The relocation centre in Qingdao was an old power station. They had to wait there until it was their turn to leave. No proper meals were provided. On a lucky day they received some water. After some months, finally it was Mr. Sakaguchi's turn to leave. By then he had lost his eyesight because of malnutrition. There were many others like him.

On the ship they were given three meals of wheat a day. His eyesight gradually returned. When he saw the blurred horizon from the deck, he realized that he had made it. Their ship arrived at Sasebo. They went through a quarantine inspection, and then headed for Fukuoka on a goods train.

The city of Fukuoka had been completely destroyed by the air raids; leaving wasteland and rubble everywhere.

When he finally reached the island, his cousin was waiting to meet him at the port. He was told then that his younger brother who had been sent to the front in Chongqing had also returned alive. But his older brother had been killed. At home his brother's wife was left widowed with her three-year-old daughter. As she was from a poor farming family, it was not possible for her to return home as there was no place for her. Thus one of the brothers had to take care of them. The younger brother who had been a teacher at elementary school before the war begged Mr. Sakaguchi to let him continue his profession. So he was left with no other choice but to become the head of the family. He had his name removed from his aunt's family register and entered in the original one. He married his sister-in-law, even though both of them were not happy about it. "Even so, I told myself that I was still better off than those who died on the battle field."

He supported his family by farming and fishing. Their married life unexpectedly worked out well and they were blessed with four children.

He would sometimes meet with veterans from his unit. Such a gathering was called Senyukai, the war-friend-association. At the gathering they almost ate or drank nothing, but instead they talked endlessly about the old days; what miserable days they had, or how lucky they were to have been able to return alive. They mourned over their comrades who had died of hunger.

Now seventy years after the war, most of the members of the association had passed away. Mr. Sakaguchi himself suffered from a stroke last September, and had minor paralysis, but he was recovering through rehabilitation. He has, however, given up farming and fishing.

"Now I just live from day to day, go to sleep at nightfall and wake up at daybreak."

Taiki – A Big Tree

My father was a fisherman until he lost his left leg from the thigh down. He was asked to help to repair the motor of his friend's boat. Old motors used to have semi-diesel engines with a flywheel, and a pull cord to start. Sometimes the cord did not draw back properly and flailed around. On such an occasion, the cord slashed my father, and cost him his leg. He couldn't continue fishing after that.

As he had a small house in Toinokuchi, he started to sell rice and other things there. My mother used to go around the island on foot, over the mountains, sometimes as far as Yunomoto, carrying on her back produce and fish to sell. It was my father's business, but it was my mother who put in the hard work.

I am the same age as Roppei, we played a lot together and were always up to no good. Roppei was the leader of our group of friends. We used to catch eels at the water gate in Toinokuchi. Sometimes, we attempted to catch them at another water gate further upstream, but ended up empty handed and bitten by crabs, big hairy ones. Eels and crabs were plentiful then.

In those days spinning tops and marbles were popular. We didn't have real marbles, so we used the stones of washnuts after taking off the shell. We also played Menko cards. We gambled with them, and if you won you would win the card of your opponent. Some boys had really nice cards with pictures of Samurai. Some would cheat by putting candle wax under their cards, so that they wouldn't turn over.

We used to love walking on stilts. They were up to three meters tall, so to help us get onto them, we sat on the stone wall over there. Stilts were made from clothes-poles, which were made of bamboo. There weren't any metal poles at that time. The best stilts were made of bamboo leftover after the Star Festival. We were very skilled, we never fell. We used to challenge each other to see who was the bravest. First, we would take our right hand off the stilt, then the left foot, finally we would touch the bottom of our left foot with our right hand while still standing on the stilts. In the beginning, we could only do this once, but after practice we were able to repeat it as many as ten times. Falling would have been a disaster as we were at roof height. Actually we used to sit on the roofs to take a rest.

We used to catch white-eye birds. We would put a white-eye bird in a box to act as a decoy to lure other birds, and cover the surrounding branches with birdlime. Birds perching on the branches would become stuck, we would try to catch them before they flew away. These were the games of our childhood.

Mr. Itami was a good teacher. He was our homeroom teacher when I was in the second year of elementary school. Mr. Itami Zenju. He was already an old grey haired man by then. Other teachers would shout aloud when they wanted pupils to assemble together. But as Mr. Itami was so old, he blew a whistle instead. Children used to make fun of him. But everyone liked him. During the war, he used to come to school wearing gaiters. He taught my parents too. He was a man of dignity.

His house was in the upper part of Taniebashi. He had a sheep and brought it to school, and told children to feed it with grass. There was a vegetable garden at school, and we were told to manure it with night soil. He taught pupils about sheep and growing vegetables. When I come to think of it, this was a part of his way of educating us. It was a good education.

I still remember what he taught us. "Suppose your house was broken into by a burglar," he would start, "how do you think he would appraise it? Where would he first look to see whether the house was well organized or not? Of course, he would look at the chest of drawers. If it was untidy with some clothes sticking out, he would feel he could take anything from the house without being noticed." Since that day, I have been careful how I organize my chest of drawers. He was indeed a good teacher.

After Mr. Itami, our homeroom teacher was Mr. Kakegawa Chukei. He was probably about twenty years old. He was very strict. He held a thinly cut bamboo stick, and would hit us with it. It was so painful. He taught us semaphore as it was wartime. I still remember how to signal "Come quickly." Then he was conscripted. "If I am ever killed, my spirit will return to Yasukuni Shrine," he said before he left. He was killed on his way to Okinawa from the mainland.

Whilst Mr. Kakegawa was still in charge of us, there was a fight between the third graders and the fourth graders. Some of the fourth graders were acting violently with a wooden gun and came into our class room and started teasing us, and a little fight broke out. Roppei was our leader. Their leader was Yu, the son of a timber dealer. Mr. Kakegawa found us fighting, "Line up facing each other. Now punch the boy in front of you. This is your punishment," he ordered. He would lose his job if he did the same thing today.

We stood face to face with our opponents and hit each

other five times each. Some hit lightly and others hit with all their might. Who was my opponent? Maybe it was Tatsu, the son of an oil maker. I hit him lightly and he hit me back the same way. But Roppei, being the leader, fought hard with Yu. I'll always remember that. The leaders became good friends after finishing school. Yu passed away this year. There was a photo of the port over there in the living room of Yu's house. That was taken by Roppei. He saw the picture in Roppei's room, and asked for it, so Roppei enlarged it for him.

My favourite memory from junior high school was when we built our own school house. We first dismantled the official residence for soldiers at Morotsu, then carried the materials to the school yard using rickshaws. It was a long arduous journey, over a hill, through a forest, weaving right, then left. We even laid the foundations ourselves. During the construction, we also made a sumo ring, too.

Another thing I remember well is the school festival when I was in the final year at junior high school. It took place at a theater in the evening. Roppei and I performed a pantomime. Other students either danced or sang. Our pantomime was the finale. I played a young Buddhist disciple and Roppei was the priest. We were dressed in proper costumes and prepared an imitation spider. The idea of the performance was that while the disciple was practicing asceticism, a spider landed on his head. It was a success and the audience roared with laughter.

We went to Sofukuji-temple in Fukuoka on a school trip. We took our own rice with us and cooked for ourselves. First we visited the Yahata steel manufacturing company as part of our study, then we went to Shimonoseki, where we visited the cold room of a large ocean fishery company known as Taiyo Gyogyo. It was the first time I had seen frozen fish. After finishing junior high school, I stayed home for about a year. I could not decide what to do. After visiting the main land on a school trip, I realized that there was a huge world out there, but on the other hand I felt responsible towards my father and his disability. Then one day a man came and asked me whether I wanted to work as an apprentice at a Japanese cake shop. I consulted my father and he said, "You should go." I didn't want to go because of my father, but in the end I was compelled to do so.

The cake shop was in Katsumoto. I walked all the way there carrying my bedding on my back, as cars were not very common at that time. It was around the time your grandfather bought a motorbike. There were only four people who owned motorbikes, the doctor, Mr. Yoshiura, Mr. Shibakyu and someone else, I forget who. At that time motorbikes were so rare that whenever we heard your grandfather pass by, we would rush to catch a glimpse of him.

At Babasaki in Katsumoto, there is a guest house called Fukuya-inn. It used to be a cake shop with the same name. They made various kinds of Japanese sweets, fresh, baked, and steamed. I was the first apprentice. Next came Kawada, and he was followed by four or five others. They were trying to expand the business, so they employed some confectioners as well.

The life of apprentice was tough. We started at five in the morning, our first job was to cook the beans. We cooked both white beans and red azuki beans, then pureed them to make anko (bean jam). It was known as kneading, and it was not easy. We apprentices kneaded anko until midday. When we thought the anko was ready, we consulted the confectioners to make sure they approved. Then we cooled it. In the afternoon we helped to make cakes. We baked Kuri-Manjyu and Kasumaki in the oven. We worked until nine in the evening.

There was a separate house for the young apprentices to sleep. On the odd occasion that we finished our work early, we would head into the town of Katsumoto to have fun.

There were quite a few sake breweries nearby such as Harada, Shimojyo and Tonokawa. We would often go to one of them to drink. In those days, there was always somewhere connected to the breweries where we could sit and enjoy ourselves drinking the breweries own brand like Tsutanokotobuki, Fukutsubaki, but not any longer.

On our days-off I used to go home by bicycle. It took quite a long time. In Seto there was a brothel called Kadono-ya. The owner would scold me whenever he saw me. He would say, "This isn't the place for you." "Think about your father and what he's been through." He wouldn't let me in however many times I tried.

Going to the brothel was expensive. There was even a song about it, "Just a peek three hundred yen, touch touch five hundred yen, one step further a thousand five hundred yen, to stay until the rooster's cry three thousand five hundred yen." The prices in the song were actually the price you had to pay.

Well, either way whether I went home or stayed out in Seto, I had to be back for work in the morning, ready to make anko. The confectioners weren't that strict on us, telling us to learn by ourselves, or "Just watch what we do."

The apprenticeship took about three years. After that we were obliged to work one year at the shop. After finishing there, I went to Ashibe to work for Hamaya, which is now a western style confectioner's. The late proprietor of the shop used to work for the post office, but for some reason or other decided to open a confectionary shop. He asked me to help him as he needed some confectioners. At that time it was a Japanese style cake shop. I worked there for about two years. After that I worked for another cake shop in Gonoura for about two years.

We used to have fun by teasing young women at the festivals or shows known as Engeikai which were held by the young men's association, and were something like a grown-up version of a school festival. Each area including Ashibe or Seto used to hold their own Engeikai. We went as often as we could as they offered an opportunity for the young men and women to meet. Engeikai usually started around seven in the evening. We would go all dressed up. An outdoor stage was prepared for the performances like Japanese dance, singing and plays. When everything was over, we would try to talk girls into letting us escort them home. I enjoyed that.

I returned home at twenty-five and opened my own shop. In those days we sold a lot of cakes and business was good. People bought special cakes for every kind of occasion, cerebration, or memorial service. Cakes were necessities then. For the annual Boy's day, we made a special set of carp shaped sweets, depicting the symbol of the day.

About one year after opening my shop, I got married.

One of my customers who came to order cake asked me if I was looking for a wife. I was surprised by his suggestion but thought why not. She was his granddaughter. I found her very attractive. She was twenty-one, five years younger than I. We got married on May fifth, Boy's day. Ironically on that day I became a man.

By the time I was thirty, my wife was able to make cakes and run the shop by herself. So I started fishing. I was a late starter, so there was a lot to learn. I learned how to find the best fishing spots by studying the mountain range in the distance. It was important to return to the same spot the following day. We had to have a knowledge of sea beds, all the troughs and all the shallows. By doing this we could ascertain where the fish might be. The modern ships are fitted with GPS systems and fish detectors, so it is just a matter of tapping in a few numbers. In those days we didn't have those. I started out with a small boat, then step by step, I bought bigger ones. Fishing became my main source of income. I still had the cake shop, but cakes were becoming less popular, and besides the food hygiene laws were becoming stricter. Even so, my wife continued the shop into her sixties when we finally closed it.

I like fishing for yellowtails the best. The way they tug on the line leaves a special sensation. But fishing yellowtails isn't so profitable. They are cheap. You can't make your living by chasing yellowtails. You have to fish squid as well. At this time of the year grunts are delicious.

I still go fishing. I leave home at five in the morning, still dark, I can't even see my hands in front of my face, but fishing starts at first light. You have to leave early, or they don't latch onto the bait. The tide changes once the day breaks. The ship I have now is four tons. Its name is Kompira-maru. Many of the ships on this island have same names, don't they? Ebisu-maru and Kompira-maru are so common. They were taken from the names of shipping gods. Everyone goes to visit Kompirasan in Shikoku, where there is a shrine dedicated to the god Kompira. In fact, I have been there three times.

I have four children, but unfortunately before them we lost two, both were boys. The first one was stillborn. The second one lived for only three days and never left the hospital. I didn't have to name the stillborn child, but I had to register a name for the second one. Thinking of a name for a dead child was the hardest thing for me. While rushing to the hospital after hearing the news, I tried hard, but couldn't think of any. Just as I arrived, I saw a big tree in front of the hospital, so I named him Taiki, meaning a big tree. I kept this to myself. I have never told anybody about this until now. As it was the second time to lose a child, my wife became so depressed. But the four children born after them grew healthy. My wife and I are still on good terms with each other. I should say I owe a lot to my wife's tolerance.

Well, in retrospect, so many things happened in my life.

Stone Walls

My father was a stone mason, who also grew rice. I started working for him when I left school. I began by practicing with the chisel. When you work with stone, there is a very particular and precise way of hitting the chisel with the hammer. You have to be very careful, if not, broken pieces can fly off, I know some stone masons with badly damaged noses.

When I was sixteen or seventeen years old, we built the stone wall of your old family clinic. It was during the war. You can look over there, and see the Maeyama mountain where the stones were brought from. We used slightly soft stones, as they were easy to carve. It took a master two and a half minutes to straighten one stone. This became the standard time allowed. After carving, they were moved slowly by carts, often blocking the road. Whenever the captain of the fortress headquarter passed on horseback on the opposite side of the road, we had to stop and salute him.

The war ended, and work became busier. We made that stone wall in Ashibe. I received my wages on payday just like other employees, but I had to give all of it back to my parents, and in return I was given some spending money.

I broke this finger when trying to move a heavy stone with my master. He lifted the stone a little too early and my hand was crushed under it. I hurried to your hospital and Dr. Hiroki said, "What do you want to do? If you want to continue working, I will have to pull back the skin and flesh to get to the bone." "Doctor, do what you have to do," I said. After the operation, my finger was numb for a while, so I didn't feel much pain. However, because of his skill, I can still move my finger.

I used to help my father with his farming, too. We planted rice in May, after which we would relax, and go to the beach and drink. We would sing songs, "Ah-iya-sahno-sa," and play Taiko-drums, "Tan, tan, tantakatan⋯," and drink some more. But nowadays all the planting is done by machine.

Well, what else did we do to enjoy ourselves? We used to go to the cinema, Shurakukan, to watch Samurai movies. As we didn't have any money to buy tickets, we crouched down and sneaked past the ticket office. When the draught brew through the auditorium, it would ruffle the screen, and the samurai's faces would sway in the wind.

During the summer, I can't remember any other pleasure than swimming. Young people today don't even know how to row a boat. We used to row out to sea, dive and swim naked. In those days there were lots of turban shells and sea urchins. But we knew not to take too many because some people's lives depended on them.

Compared to us, the fishermen were more quick-tempered. They used to shout out, "Oi, plebs." "Who are you talking to?" Around Bon festival fights often broke out. We used to hang around outside Kawazoe Store, wearing our yukatas with their sleeves rolled up. We wore wooden geta footwear which made a rattling noise as we walked. Our enemies would say, "Oi, come over here." Then we would say, "What do you want?" and the fighting would start. Whenever we went to Ashibe, we carried something sharp like a knife, just in case. We shortened our swords by breaking them in two.

In those days there were so many fish and fishing was much more profitable. So I gave up my job as a stonemason and started working for Mr. Kuwamitsu, the head fisherman who owned three large fishnets. The catches were big. Each cast of the net brought in more and more fish. It became too much for us to handle. We made so much money.

Kissing became popular after the war. I went dancing in the evening. I would put my hands around a girl's waist and kiss her. I loved it. I used to go to Higashi-Nakasu in Hakata, because there was no place to dance on the island. I had a girlfriend in Fukuoka, her name was Yamazaki Matsue. I used to sleep at her place in 3-chome in Higashi-Nakasu. She was a geisha, and always carried a shamisen with her. I used to visit her once a month. I had earned plenty of money from the fishing. I took a ship from Katsumoto.

Ultimately, however, it turns out I was a farm boy, my temperament was different from that of the fishermen. Fishing was like gambling. After sometime I left Mr. Kuwamitsu's, and returned to growing rice and making stone walls. I married a woman introduced to me by a matchmaker. At that time marriage for love wasn't so common. I had two children.

I really worked hard. We built all the stone walls around Aoshima Park. I enjoyed laying stones. Now walls are mostly made of concrete, stone walls are no longer wanted and consequently we weren't needed any more, so I quit.

Now I spend most of my time at a day care home.

If you go to Maeyama quarry, you can probably still find some unused stones.

Oh, how I used to chisel away at the stones. Young people now wouldn't be able to do that!

Medicine Bottles

What stands out in my memory is the little lane from my village Morotsu to school. It was narrow, windy, and steep. It was so troublesome especially on a rainy day. To make things worse, I had to walk barefooted as my family was so poor.

My old grandmother had a weak chest, so I had to go and get medicine for her on my way to and from school. It was my responsibility. It meant I missed a lot of lessons and other school activities. I often had to visit your grandfather's clinic in Sangenjaya. I had to get two types of medicine for my grandmother, some powdered wrapped in paper and some in a bottle. I had to walk through the forest for two hours to get to the clinic. As the clinic was always crowded, I just left the empty bottle there to be filled, then headed for school. By the time I reached school it was already noon. I had missed most of the morning classes. I had to leave school early to pick up the medicine at the clinic when it was ready. But again with so many patients, I had to wait my turn. Finally I could head for home.

The old road to Morotsu used to be so lonely, not like it is today. It used to be so narrow, about the width of a tatami mat, just enough for a man to pass. After the sun set, I sometimes walked home crying. Finding myself in the depth of the forest, I felt so alone, a different feeling from being scared.

My grandmother passed away, then my father fell ill. So I had to keep going to the clinic to get medicine, until finally my father passed away. He died when I was twenty-five.

As soon as I finished elementary school, I started working in the fields. I grew wheat, soybeans, vegetables, and water melons. I took them to sell in Seto but the roads were so bad. I had to go up and down and around the mountains. When my father fell ill, it was my responsibility to run the household as I was the first born son and had seven younger brothers and sisters.

I also went fishing on a small rowing boat. The catch was much better during the winter, from around November to March or April. Mostly cuttlefish. I fished at night in the dark. I left around seven and came back around eleven. I fished alone. Some men used to take their sons. Everyone here lives off the sea and the land. Cuttlefish were cleaned and then hung to be dried. Such work was done the following morning. The women would help as the work would take all morning. Then I would go to the field to farm. In the winter we grew only vegetables. We planted wheat at the end of February, and harvested it in May. Soy beans were harvested in June.

I used to dive for abalones and turban shells when I was younger. I would dive five or six fathoms deep without wearing any diving apparatus. Nowadays divers wear wet suits, but then it was too cold in the winter, so I dived only in the summer.

It was 1941 when the Pacific War began, wasn't it? It was the year I finished school. The Navy Officials suddenly appeared and said, "We are going to build barracks here. This place is going to be confiscated." They confiscated the whole area I showed you earlier and beyond that too. It was a fine place with a wonderful view. They took away our fields and our rice paddies. They said the land would be used for soldiers. There was nothing we could do. At that time everyone was at war and didn't have any say in the matter. Fortunately I had some other land, and I was able to feed my family.

The land was later returned along with the remains of a concrete water tower and the foundations of the barracks. They are quite a nuisance. I have often asked the local officials to have them removed, but without success.

I got married at twenty-six. I feel embarrassed to say it but the bride was my cousin. In those days you could not choose your partner. It was decided for you. So I married my cousin.

When I was seventy, my boat was hit from behind by a bigger squid fishing boat, and it sank. The captain of the ship had been sleeping. Because I was a diver, I was able to survive somehow. I could open my eyes even under water. My boat had sunk and my fishing days ended.

I am now eighty-nine years old. There are three women of my age still alive around here, but I am the only man. You see, I used to walk a lot in my childhood, maybe that exercise held me in good stead. I really walked a lot. I am not sure what is good for me, but I still go to work in the fields now. Thirty years ago, a new rord was built. It made going to other places a lot easier.

Well, I really worked hard. That may be the reason I have managed to live this long.

Flying Alone

It takes two and a half hours by ferry from Fukuoka to Iki-island, and only an hour by jetfoil. You used to be able to fly but not any longer, because it stopped making any economic sense.

I was probably seven years old when I took an air plane by myself for the first time. I was supposed to fly with my brother to spend our summer holiday with our grandparents on the island, but for some reason I had to fly alone. My mother saw me off at the boarding gate in Fukuoka Airport. A cabin attendant led me by the hand onto a propeller plane.

The flight took less than twenty minutes. From almost the moment it took off, it started to descend. The arrangement was that I was handed over to my aunt who was supposed to be waiting at the arrival gate. But for some reason, I found myself left alone in the arrival lobby of the island airport. My aunt was nowhere to be seen. I was so shy and could not bring myself to ask the airport staff for help. When I come to think of it now, it was silly of me.

Not knowing what to do, I just stood there peering outside. The side of the lobby that looked over the parking lot was made of glass, and the dazzling light of the afternoon sun blinded my eyes. Squinting, I continued to gaze outside. Turning around I saw a long shadow of myself cast against the floor. I stood between the light and the shadow.

*

A short story of mine was published in a literary magazine for the first time last year. It was based on my memories with my grandparents on the island. Six years after I had set my mind on becoming a writer, my manuscript was finally printed. It received a mixed response. Some praised it, but others said tilting their heads, "Well, I'm not sure." "It lacks perception." That made me think.

About a month after the magazine was out, I received a call from a local writer, a leading figure in the literary world. His old age has not affected his clear and scathing tongue. His critical eye (and perception) had not been blurred by time. I have read most of his books and admired his writing. We were going to meet to talk about my story. I felt nervous but at the same time excited, for I was going to learn what he thought about my writing whether I liked it or not. I hurried in the drizzling to a coffee shop where we were going to meet.

As I opened the door of the coffee shop, I found the writer already there with a coffee. "I've read your short story," he started without any preface. "Your style isn't fashionable, and it's not an easy read for everyone." He raised his cup to his mouth, and continued. "But never mind about novels written in a popular style. You must not end that short story there, you should tell the story not just about your grandparents but also other people living on the island. You should meet them, listen to them, and record what they say." "Collect memories." "Collect voices." "The importance is in the detail," he stressed. "You don't have to be part of the story. Record the island's details."

People entrusted their memories to my pen and a tape recorder. Naturally not every story was a pleasant one. Some of them were painful, full of anxiety.

To listen to others means to share a part of their lives.

The difficult memories from my past allowed me to get closer to the speakers and they in turn reveal their stories to me.

*

The seven-year-old boy at the airport lobby did not have, needless to say, much of a past or many memories to speak of. He would never have known or thought that there would be countless stories waiting to be told dotted around the island. He was only flustered staring outside of the window.

Suddenly I saw the advertising board of a watch store owned by one of my distant relatives, the shop phone number was written in the corner. I had a few coins in my pocket. I went to the phone box and dialed. Why did I call the watch store? I simply couldn't remember the number of my grandparents or of my aunt. I did not want to call home. Was it an attempt to save my honor as the second son? I explained to my uncle, half in tears, what had happened. He said, "Oh, that is too bad," and then started to laugh aloud. I could not help laughing despite myself. Laughing, I realized that the nightmare situation I was in only a few moments ago was actually oh so trivial. If you laugh, you can overcome most hardships. At least that was what I felt at that time. I was about to have a wonderful summer. And over time I would learn that even airlines can disappear.

"Stay where you are. I'll be there right away."

I felt so relieved and hung up the receiver.